D.J. felt Nick behind her, the warmth of his body burning through her clothes, felt his hands moving on her arms as he pulled her back against him. Part of her wanted to turn and throw her arms around him. The other part strained away from him.

"I never did feed you tonight," he whispered against her ear.

"Not food." She was incapable of anything but a whisper either. "But something I needed much more."

She stared up at him, warring with the warmth she felt, which wanted to answer the desire she saw in his eyes, and a cold, hard core within her, which hissed insidiously that she had no right to feel this pleasure.

ABOUT THE AUTHOR

Modean Moon shares a common interest with
the heroine of this book—they both deal in oil
leases. Modean is a petroleum landman and
travels extensively throughout the Midwest
on various assignments. Originally from
Oklahoma City, Modean now lives in Poteau,
Oklahoma. This is her first published novel.

Dare
to Dream

MODEAN MOON

Harlequin Books

TORONTO • NEW YORK • LONDON
AMSTERDAM • PARIS • SYDNEY • HAMBURG
STOCKHOLM • ATHENS • TOKYO • MILAN

Published November 1984

First printing September 1984

ISBN 0-373-16077-1

Printed in Canada

Chapter One

D.J. awoke on the carpet at the foot of her bed, the screams from her nightmare echoing through the silent room, her hands outstretched to the door that was no longer there.

"No," she whimpered. "Not again. Please, not again."

Instinctively she began the exercises with her hands that she had done for so many months. Clench, grip, extend. Clench, grip, extend. She repeated the exercises, no longer needing the rubber balls she had once squeezed as she tried to hold on to her sanity, until she felt her trembling ease, and she slumped against the bed, exhausted and drenched.

She looked at her hands. In the morning light, filtering through drawn drapes, they looked older than her twenty-eight years warranted. It was strange, she thought gratefully, how few persons ever noticed that the aging was really scarring.

She leaned her head against the bed with a moan. She might as well think about it. It wasn't going to leave her alone until she did. Five years ago today—a dozen lifetimes and yet only yesterday; added day by

day on the calendar, it had been five years since her life
was torn apart.

She pulled herself to her feet and paced into the
bathroom where she wrestled out of her sodden nightgown, turned the shower on full force, and let the
water beat against her.

She was lucky, they'd told her when she left the hospital. There would be minor scarring—only on the
hands, and a little along the hairline, easily concealable.
Her hair was already growing back when she left.
Darker, now an auburn, the red only glinted when
struck by sunlight. Lucky. Lucky. When all she'd
lost—when all she'd lost—was everything. Nothing
tangible remained as evidence of the love she and Rob
had shared, not even her wedding ring, lost in the confusion of the emergency room.

"Is that enough?" she whispered aloud as she toweled her hair and reached for the dryer. "Or do I have
to keep going over it and picking at it?"

"It's enough," she said in a suddenly calm voice.

She made quick work of her makeup, a little cover-
up feathered into her hairline and onto the backs of her
hands, a touch of mascara and lip gloss. She parted her
hair in the middle, brought wings down on each side of
her face, and caught the length of it back in a smooth
knot on her nape. The style was severe, but it helped to
counteract the impression of youthful helplessness in-
spired by large blue eyes and generous, softly curved
lips, by providing a somber frame for her heart-shaped
face, and it camouflaged the almost invisible scars.

Soon she was inspecting her image in the full-length
mirror on her closet door. "Welcome back to the real
world, D.J.," she said wryly.

She saluted the image reflected back at her, that of a composed, professional-looking woman in a teal-blue silk blouse, beige linen skirt and jacket, and trim high-heeled pumps that added sometimes needed stature to her petitely scaled five feet four inches.

"You'll do fine," she said with determination.

She picked up her purse, looked regretfully at the empty coffeepot sitting on the kitchen counter, shrugged, and started out the door. D.J. knelt down for the newspaper and tossed it inside the apartment. No time for that, either, this morning. She felt something soft and furry brushing against her legs.

"Are you back?" she asked with exasperation of a small bundle of black-and-white fluff. "I told you to go away, kitten," she said, softening her voice. "Now scat! There's nothing here for you."

She thought of the sterile apartment she had just left. *There's nothing here for me either* flitted through her mind. Heavy traffic in south Tulsa required that she concentrate on her driving, though, and by the time she reached the interstate highway that looped the city, she had banished her traitorous thoughts.

On a whim she turned onto the interstate and whipped over to Riverside Drive. It would take longer to get to her parking garage once she reached downtown, but even in traffic there was a calming quality about driving along the river, seeing the bikers and joggers on the paths in river parks, and winding through an older part of town that exuded an aura of an easier, less harried time.

When she reached the beautifully maintained building that housed the law offices where she worked, she found Marcie already in her alcove, her pert, curly head bent over the typewriter, fingers flying over the keys. Marcie looked up when D.J. walked into the alcove.

"You've got a nine o'clock appointment," she said, flashing an impish grin.

D.J. dropped her purse on Marcie's desk and shrugged out of her jacket. "Who set that one up?"

"None other than Mr. Merriweather himself."

"Who, and why?" D.J. asked, reaching for the thermal server.

"Sorry, D.J. I haven't had a chance to go for the coffee yet. The why is easy. Nick Sanders has apparently thrown a gasket over your last title opinion."

"I don't blame him," D.J. said dryly.

"Anyway, he called demanding to see Henry Slayton, who of course is still on vacation."

"Of course."

"So he went straight to the top, and Mr. Merriweather has assured him that you will explain everything to his complete satisfaction."

D.J.'s delighted laugh broke from her. "How do you manage to learn all these tidbits of information? Never mind," she said as Marcie opened her mouth to answer. "I don't want to know. Just tell me who he's sending."

"The great man," Marcie pronounced exaggeratedly, "is coming himself."

"That's terrific, Marcie. All I need is an irate client the first thing this morning. Tell me, office ears, is there anything else I need to know about him?"

"Only that he's thirty-seven, he's been divorced for years, and the women in word processing say that he is one gorgeous hunk."

D.J. could only shake her head and smile at the

younger woman. "Did they also tell you when the Miller contract would be ready?"

"It's promised by eight forty-five."

"Good." She draped her jacket across Marcie's chair and picked up the thermal server. "If you'll get that and the Sanders file, I'll take care of the important things."

It might be possible, D.J. mused as she hurried toward her office with the coffee tray, to keep herself busy enough that she wouldn't have time to think today.

She rounded the corner into her hallway, and all musing screamed to a halt. For once the women in word processing had not been extravagant in their praise. It had to be Nick Sanders standing in the hall between her office and Marcie's alcove—at least six feet three of dark, rugged impatience.

Something—appraisal perhaps—flickered in his green eyes as she slid the tray onto the alcove's passthrough counter and reached across to answer Marcie's persistently buzzing intercom.

"Marcie's desk," she answered, only to have the receptionist's agitated voice confirm her suspicions.

"Nick Sanders is on his way back there. He refused to wait any longer."

"That's all right, Jeanne. He's here now."

No, he was not the type to wait patiently, D.J. thought as she glanced at the man looming above her. Her job of explaining the problems in his latest contract and soothing his ruffled temper wasn't going to be made any easier by keeping him waiting.

"Won't you go on in, Mr. Sanders, and have a chair?" She nodded toward her office door as she picked up the coffee tray. "It will be a few minutes before your files are brought up."

She followed him into the office and slid the tray onto the visitor's side of her desk.

"For me?" he asked, pulling himself out of his thoughts for only a moment. "Thanks." He poured himself a cup of coffee, turned from her, and walked to the glass wall overlooking the city.

D.J.'s eyebrow shot up at the obvious dismissal, but she bit back an angry retort. It wouldn't do her any good to snap at him. She started out to Marcie's alcove to gather her things but paused at the door and looked back at her client. Her client? She shook her head. Not hers, thank God. After four and a half years with Merriweather, Pratt, Widlyme and Tanner, she was intimately familiar with the legal aspects of his business transactions, but this was the first time she had even seen the man, let alone been entrusted with dealing with him.

She studied him quietly from across the room. Rich, dark hair, almost black, worn carelessly long, hinted at waves as it fell to his collar. He wore work clothes—khaki slacks that hugged long powerful legs and a short-sleeved shirt that exposed muscular arms. He was bronzed by years in the weather, honed to a lean perfection by physical labor, and only caribou boots, a slim gold watch, and an unmistakable air about the way he held himself gave any indication of his success.

Outlined against the glass wall of her sixteenth-floor office, suspended against the skyline of Tulsa—skyscrapers rising among the terra-cotta-trimmed art deco buildings of the twenties and the Gothic Renaissance buildings of the first rush of oil money—he seemed a part of the new steel and glass. And well he should, she realized. He was building it.

D.J. slid into the second guest chair. He turned at the slight noise, a question in his eyes, and reached for the server to pour himself more coffee.

"I haven't had my coffee yet," she said softly. "Will you pour a cup for me, too?"

A hint of a smile played about his lips as he did so and handed it to her. "Marcie, is it?" he asked as his gaze, no longer hooded and introspective, inspected her, missing no detail as it moved up her long, hose-clad legs, the linen skirt outlining trim hips and waist as she lounged in the chair, the silk shirt that draped softly over small breasts, to rest finally on her face.

"No, I'm not Marcie," she said. She never enjoyed the inspections, but she had realized that there was nothing she could do to stop them. Only after they had been completed could she begin to counteract that first sensual appraisal by her competence and ability.

"You're filling in for her, then?" he asked. Speculation softened the impatience in his eyes, and she saw green lights sparking to life in their depths. He obviously liked what he saw, D.J. realized with a start. It was time to get down to business.

"No. Mr. Sanders, I—" she began, but a soft tap at the doorway interrupted her.

Marcie, no longer flip and joking, came quietly into the office. "These are the files you requested, Miss Simms. Do you need anything else at this time?" she asked softly.

D.J. took the files from her. "No, Marcie. That will be all for now."

The woman nodded and left the room as quietly as she had entered, closing the door gently behind her.

"Miss Simms?" Nick Sanders asked incredulously. "D. J. Simms?"

"Yes," she said coolly as she rose and walked behind the desk to her chair.

"You're a woman," he said flatly.

"You've been aware of that for several minutes, Mr. Sanders."

"Yes, I have been aware of that," he admitted, his voice edged with repressed anger. "But I was not aware that you were the person responsible for this title opinion." He pulled the folded papers from his pocket and flung them on the desk.

"I understand that you've taken exception to my opinion," she said, her voice devoid of emotion, waiting for the right opportunity to begin to appease him and finally to convince him that his interests were being protected.

"You're damned right I've taken exception to it. I've done the impossible. I've contracted for a rig to start drilling this well six weeks from now. I have an iron-clad contract with Sam Wilson to buy one hundred percent of the leasehold in a six-hundred-and-forty-acre drilling unit directly offsetting the biggest gas well in western Oklahoma, and you're telling me that not only do I not have one hundred percent of the working interest in the leases, I have less than half."

When he paused for breath, D.J. interjected softly, "I believe one of the reasons you retain this firm is to advise you of possible legal complications, Mr. Sanders. That's what I've done."

"I want to talk to Slayton."

D.J. sighed and then swiveled her chair around to the credenza behind her. Opening a door, she reached in and drew forth a stack of abstracts, compilations of every document that had been placed of record in the County Clerk's office concerning the land his leases encompassed.

"He won't be back until a week from Monday," she said as she placed the abstracts on the desk and slid them toward him, "and I understand that time is important. Even by messenger it would take several days to have these delivered to him in the British Virgin Islands and returned." She looked at him steadily. "For you, he probably would interrupt his vacation to read the abstracts, but when he did, he would tell you the same thing I have already told you. It would be to your advantage, Mr. Sanders, if we devoted that time to attempting to solve the problems that exist rather than arguing about whether those problems really exist."

"It would be to my advantage," he said with a ring of steel in his voice, "to have the opinion of someone other than a half-grown girl just out of law school. There's too much riding on this for me to have to depend on your immaturity and inexperience."

D.J. forced herself to show no reaction to his outburst. Instead she leaned back in her chair and swiveled it slightly so that she could look out the glass wall toward the trio of steel and glass towers that rose from behind the Williams Center, overshadowing it, tying North Tulsa with the heart of downtown that lay south of the railroad.

"You're familiar with the Brady Center," she said, still looking at the buildings.

"Of course I am," he snapped.

Of course. She had expected his terse answer. She knew it had been his foresight that had enabled him to buy acres of slum property and develop the project, a skillful blending of inner city apartments, luxury offices, restaurants, and specialty shops.

"When I first started with Merriweather-Pratt," she said emotionlessly, "those buildings were still on paper."

"You've been here that long?" he asked.

She nodded, still looking at the buildings, remembering her first assignment with the Tulsa firm. "It was I who discovered that two heirs to one of the city lots in the center of your construction site had been omitted from an early quiet title suit. It was I who located those heirs. And it was I who negotiated the purchase of their interests in the lot so that excavation could begin. So," she said with a grim smile, "appearance to the contrary, I am not without experience."

He appraised her again, but not sensually this time. This time she recognized a no-nonsense, clear-eyed, shrewd assessment of her business sense.

"You're the one who pulled that deal through?" he asked.

She nodded and saw the reluctant admiration in his eyes.

"You did a good job," he said.

"I know."

When a smile broke across his face, softening its harsh lines, she opened the folder in front of her. "Now let me explain where we stand and what your options are."

Quickly she outlined her basic objections to the leases in question and went over the clauses in the escrow contract that protected him. Now that he was over his initial anger, he easily grasped the problems she showed him, and his questions concerning them were so perceptive they surprised her, until she remembered that he was no stranger to title law or to oil and gas law.

When they covered the last point, he poured the remainder of the coffee into their cups, lit a cigarette, and leaned back in his chair.

"You do your homework, lady."

"It's my job, Mr. Sanders."

"Sam Wilson insists that the leases are good and that it's your title opinion that's faulty."

"Sam Wilson has a lot to gain if he can convince you of that."

"He won't, but he's going to give it one more try. This time I'll be a little better prepared to meet his arguments." He stared at her over the rim of his coffee cup. "I'd feel better about it, though, if you were present during the discussion."

D.J. studied the folder in her hand. As casual as it might sound, she recognized that this was high praise indeed from a man as independent and self-assured as Nick Sanders.

"I'd be happy to meet with you," she said. "If you'll let me know when you set up the appointment, I'll schedule my time so that I can be there."

"Good," he said, stubbing out his cigarette and rising from the chair. "I'll pick you up at six-thirty tonight. What's your address?"

D.J. glanced up at him in stunned silence before finding her voice. "What?"

"I'm meeting him for dinner tonight at seven. I'll pick you up at six-thirty. What's your address?"

"But I meant—I mean—"

He looked steadily down at her while she stammered, and then he crossed to the credenza behind her desk. He picked up the telephone book and scanned the pages, noting her address. "Which apartment?"

"Two fifty-four," she answered automatically to the authority in his voice.

"Fine. Six-thirty." He started toward the door.

She stopped him as he reached for the doorknob. "Mr. Sanders," she asked, once again in control of her voice and thoughts, "how badly do you want this drilling prospect?"

He spoke evenly. "Enough to sink a couple of million dollars of my own money into the hole."

"Enough to take it if you can only get forty-five percent of the leasehold and no guarantee that you'll be able to drill before your leases expire?" she asked.

"I'll make that decision by seven o'clock."

"I would appreciate it if you would let me know before we meet Mr. Wilson."

He nodded in acknowledgement of her request.

"One other thing," she said. "I live in a large apartment complex. My apartment is—"

"I'm familiar with the area, counselor. I believe I can find it." His lips twitched in a half smile.

Only then did she remember that one of his smaller holdings was the sprawling apartment complex where she lived. He wasn't only her client; he was also her landlord.

"Oh." She felt a flush creeping up her neck. "I guess you can."

After Nick Sanders left, D.J. stacked his files to return to Marcie and began putting away the abstracts. As she slid them toward her, a nagging sixth sense within her again told her something was wrong. She felt it. She'd felt it from the moment she had been given this assignment.

She flipped through the top abstract to the certificate on the last page. It was dated less than a month ago. She wished she could put her finger on one thing that could cause her discomfort, but she couldn't. It was the same feeling she had had about the city lot under the Brady Center. It was the same feeling she had had too many times, with good reason, to disregard it now. Perhaps a little more homework was in order. She swiveled her chair around to face the telephone and punched out the number of the abstract company in that distant western Oklahoma town.

Later, responding to a hesitant tap on her door, she raised her head from the microphone into which she was dictating. Her frown eased into a smile as Marcie stepped into the office with a stack of folders in her hand.

"It's after twelve. Do you mind if I go to lunch now?"

"No, go ahead," D.J. told her. She indicated toward her dictation unit. "I'll have a tape on your desk when you return. I need it transcribed before I leave tonight."

"Sure thing," Marcie said with a grin. D.J. never ceased to be amazed. The woman was unflappable, experienced, and more than competent, and she'd never know how she'd had the good fortune to draw her from the steno pool as her secretary.

Marcie handed her the folders and a handful of papers. "Here are the Miller contract, your phone messages, and the mail you didn't get this morning. Do you want me to bring you a sandwich?''

"No. That's okay. Enjoy your lunch. You're going to have your work cut out for you this afternoon."

D.J. glanced at the files before returning to her dictation. Marcie wasn't the only one who would be busy that day. But hadn't that been what she wanted?

Chapter Two

As D.J. inched her way homeward in the late afternoon traffic, she wished she had taken Marcie up on her offer to bring her a sandwich. An apple from the coffee room vending machine at three o'clock hadn't satisfied her growing hunger at the time. It certainly wasn't satisfying it now.

There was one advantage to working late, she thought as she waited in the backed up traffic for a car far ahead to complete a left turn. At least at the time she usually made this drive, most of the homeward-bound vehicles had completed their journeys.

Her glance strayed to the clock on the dashboard. A quarter of six. She was going to have to hurry to be ready by the time Nick Sanders picked her up. She felt the beginnings of irritation growing at the surrounding cars and forced it back. They were trapped the same as she. Getting angry wouldn't get her home any faster.

She took a deep breath and forced herself to relax. She was in a lovely neighborhood. When not in a hurry, she enjoyed this stretch of South Peoria Avenue. Impressive estates lined the east side of the street. Stately older homes graced several blocks down tree-lined intersecting streets leading to the west.

She felt the tension leaving her body and a lethargic patience creeping over her as her glance played over the surrounding yards, until a picture from her past flashed clearly in front of her eyes, jolting her upright. Although most of the time she never knew what caused these moments of instant recall, this time she had no doubt. An ancient dogwood tree stood in full bloom across the street, each blood-tipped white petal standing out in relief against the dull red brick of the two-story house behind it.

There had been a dogwood in their backyard, and the picture seared through the years, blinding with its clarity—a stop-action photograph of a two-year-old Bobby, his eyes dancing with pleasure, holding a double handful of dogwood blossoms toward her.

"Don't think about that now," she said raggedly as she clenched the steering wheel.

A car horn sounded impatiently behind her, and it finally penetrated her consciousness that now she held up traffic. She eased her foot onto the accelerator. *Just think about getting home. Think about what you're going to say to Nick Sanders. Think about how Sam Wilson is going to react. Think about how you're going to make it through the rest of this day. And night.*

She was dressed and waiting when Nick Sanders arrived, but just barely. After a quick shower, she had dressed in a mauve silk blouse and an ivory linen suit with a softly gathered skirt. In deference to the evening, she added eye shadow, blusher, and a light cologne to the limited makeup she wore, but she made certain she did not alter the image she had long ago adopted. This was to be a business encounter, not a social engagement.

She glanced confidently around her when she heard his knock on the door, thankful that Wednesday was the day Mrs. Jennings cleaned. The one-bedroom apartment was spotless.

She composed an impersonal smile as she opened the door. "Mr. Sanders—" The smile froze on her face, and she found herself without words. Gone was the khaki-clad workman of the morning. The thought that ran irrelevantly through her mind was if the women in word processing could see him now they wouldn't be able to talk about anything else for a week. Impeccably dressed in an obviously hand-tailored dark suit, he would not be mistaken for a common laborer—a common anything. His bronze coloring, accented by the white of his shirt, could no longer be attributed to weathering. It called forth pictures of long, lazy days in the sun. The silk blended wool of his jacket draped flawlessly over his broad shoulders but could not hide their inherent strength. Green lights danced in his eyes as he looked down at her, and the harsh line of his mouth softened in a smile exposing dazzlingly white teeth.

"May I come in, or are you ready to leave?"

She realized she must be gawking like a schoolgirl and mentally shook herself for her lack of poise.

"Please come in," she said. "We have a few things to discuss before we join Mr. Wilson."

She could tell that he took a quick note of her furnishings as he crossed to the couch and sat down, although his words made no mention of his impression.

"You want to know what I've decided about the prospect."

"Yes."

He glanced at the low table in front of the couch. "You don't smoke, do you?"

"Why, no," she said, puzzled at his abrupt change of subject. No. She didn't. Not anymore.

"Do you, by any chance, have an ashtray?" he asked, taking cigarettes and a practical lighter from his pocket.

Why should it bother her? she wondered. He'd smoked in her office. But still she hesitated before she went into the kitchenette and selected a saucer for him. When she placed it in front of him, he was staring absently around the room.

"I'm always amazed when I visit in one of these apartments," he said. "The unit itself is designed without personality so that the tenant can make his own statement. I was trying to decide on the way over here what kind of a statement you would make in your home."

"Did you?" she asked.

"No. I was hedging my bets between suede, chrome and glass, or printed chintz and Chippendale."

What he refrained from saying, D.J. realized, was that even furnished, her apartment remained impersonal. It had been decorated as a model, and when she leased it, she also made arrangements with the furniture-leasing company to retain what it had chosen as suitable decor. She had not added to it nor changed the location of one picture. What she refrained from saying was that the impersonality he detected *was* her statement. She couldn't become too attached to the apartment so long as it remained that way.

"Do you have a good reason for requesting me to tell you my decision now?"

"I didn't ask out of idle curiosity." She spoke carefully as she acknowledged to herself that probably only a handful of persons would dare to question what he was going to do in a given situation. "If I am to take an active part in the discussion, I need to be sure that I don't inadvertently say something that would work against what you really want to do. Even if you only want me to answer direct questions, I need to know in which direction you're leaning so that I can phrase my answer appropriately."

He exhaled heavily and leaned back against the soft cushions of the sofa. "I want it. You asked if I would take forty-five percent of it with no guarantee that I'd be able to drill. There are no guarantees in the oil patch, counselor, and I don't require one here. What I do require is some indication that arrangements can be made to drill during the term of my leases. Otherwise, I'd just be donating several hundred thousand dollars to Sam Wilson, and I see absolutely no reason for me to do that."

"How well do you know Sam Wilson?" she asked.

"Not well. I've seen him at the Petroleum Club and on the golf course a few times, and I've been to a couple of cocktail parties he's also attended."

"Do you know anyone he's done business with?"

"Only a couple of drilling funds. No one that I deal with on a regular basis. Why?"

D.J. picked up her purse from the desk near the door. Inside the purse were two envelopes. She took out the one with Nick Sanders's name on it and handed him a typed sheet of paper from within the envelope.

"This is your copy of the demands I propose we set

forth for Mr. Wilson. I don't think that he will be able to meet them."

As Nick scanned the page, his brow furrowed, and when he reached the bottom of the sheet, he looked up at her intently. "This is pretty tough, lady. It calls for complete cancellation of the escrow contract if he can't perform in thirty days. What about my options to try to clean up this mess or to pick up a part of the package?"

D.J. handed him a second closely typed page. She watched as he read it and his expression changed from curiosity to disbelief. When he looked up at her this time, his mouth was again set in a harsh slash, and his eyes reflected a cold rage that, even though not directed at her, sent a shiver down the back of her neck.

"Who knows about this?" he asked in a voice that matched the expression in his eyes.

"It came from various sources. Only you and I, and my secretary, have seen the pieces put together."

"No one," he ground out the words, "makes a fool of Nick Sanders."

"No one has," she assured him quickly. "And although it does appear that Mr. Wilson has tried, there is a chance that both of us have drawn the wrong conclusion from these facts."

His clenched fist struck the sofa.

She spoke softly. "Why don't we reserve judgment until after we talk with him?"

Nick shook his head silently and looked up at her. "You're right," he admitted reluctantly. "Why did you do this? Technically, your job was over when you wrote the title opinion. Why did you keep digging when you didn't have to?"

"It didn't feel right," she said simply. "Are you ready to go now? It's getting late."

He shrugged himself to his feet and stared down at her. "You look too damned competent."

"What?"

"I'm serious. The man obviously thinks he's pulled something over on me. If I show up with you looking the way you do, he'll be on his guard."

Disappointment tugged at her as she realized that she had been looking forward to joining forces with the man standing in front of her in a battle of wits with the unknown Sam Wilson.

"I don't have to go with you," she said, hiding that disappointment. "You're certainly capable of handling anything that comes up."

"That's not what I meant," he said, studying her intently. "Would you mind taking down your hair?"

Nick continued to study her as slowly she unpinned the smooth coil at the nape of her neck and shook out her heavy mane of hair, fluffing it forward around her face as she did. He smiled approval at the mass of waves falling about her shoulders.

"Now the jacket."

She tried to read the expression in his eyes as she unbuttoned the jacket and slipped out of it. He was seeing her as a woman again, that much she could tell. She waited while he crossed the two short steps separating them. His fingers brushed feather light against her skin as he unbuttoned the next button of her shirt, and she trembled, but she could not tell whether it was from fear, or anticipation, or simply the almost forgotten feeling of having a man's hands touching her.

He took the jacket from her and draped it over her shoulders. "It's chilly outside," he said, resting his hands on her arms as he looked deeply into her eyes. "You'll need this. And you need a name. I can't call you Miss Simms, and I'll be damned if I'll call anyone as beautiful as you are now D.J. What is your name?"

Her throat was dry, her mouth was dry, but she was unable to swallow, unable to do anything but meet the probing intensity of his gaze. "Danielle," she whispered.

"Danielle." He tasted the sound of it.

"Did anyone ever call you Dani?"

The mood shattered. "Almost everyone," she said tensely. "But that was a long time ago."

For a moment he seemed disappointed by her answer, but he grinned at her. "Then Dani it is," he said lightly. "And if you let so much as one 'Mr. Sanders' slip from your pretty lips tonight, I will plant my toe in the middle of your shin."

She grinned back at him. "A discreetly placed foot under the table? I've heard about that method of warning someone to silence. I'll be careful."

"Are you ever anything else?"

They were told that Sam Wilson had not yet arrived when they reached Lynde's, the supper club on the top floor of the tallest of the three Brady Center towers. The maitre d' ushered them to a round table a few steps up from a small dance floor and against a windowed wall overlooking the lights of the city. The table waited for three, the chairs evenly spaced around it, but with no apparent effort Nick seated her and himself side by side so that there was a visible barrier in the distance between them and the chair Sam Wilson would occupy.

A combo across the room played subdued, romantic music, reminiscent of the era of big bands.

"What would you like to drink?" Nick asked as he helped her with her jacket.

"Nothing, thank you," she murmured as she settled into her chair. "I don't drink."

He toyed with the cut crystal water goblet in front of him before asking slowly, "Do you have problems with it, or do you just prefer not to?"

Problems? What a strange question for him to ask her. The only problem she had was that alcohol relaxed the tight hold she kept on her emotions and let too many unwanted images float through her mind.

"I just prefer not to," she said, smiling hesitantly.

"Then humor me. I want Wilson to feel free to drink as much as he wants."

The first sip of Chablis sent pleasant tingles through her arms and shoulders before difusing warmth throughout her body. She toyed with her glass while the waiter accepted the news that they would not be ordering dinner until the third member of their party arrived, removed the menus, and returned with a tray of appetizers.

She assuaged her hunger by nibbling on the boiled shrimp and chunks of flaky crabmeat. The wine warmed and soothed her. Music from the thirties and forties lulled her. The lights of Tulsa spread out before her like millions of stars. As she sat close to Nick, exchanging only small talk, skirting around the edges of any topic that threatened to become too personal, something stirred within her that had lain dormant for

years—an enjoyment of something other than her
work, a tentative feeling of pride in her femininity,
and, not the least, pleasure in the company of the at-
tractive, attentive man beside her.

Dani, he had renamed her, and for now that's who
she would be. Not D.J. Not for a while longer.

The arrival of Sam Wilson thirty minutes later
snapped her back to reality.

"Sorry I'm late." Wilson waved the waiter away with
a command for a gin and tonic, and his eyes flicked
over Dani in shrewd assessment. "I thought you were
bringing your lawyer."

"Yes. And isn't Dani a pleasant surprise?" Nick
said, not denying the man's wrong assumption, but not
actually saying anything to confirm it. "Dani, this is
Sam Wilson."

"How do you do, Mr. Wilson." She studied him sur-
reptitiously. Compared to Nick, he was a small man,
although he must have been five ten or eleven. He
wore a dark suit as carefully tailored as the one Nick
wore and tastefully expensive jewelry. There was nothing obvious about his appearance to cause her to mis-
trust him, but she detected a thinly veiled hunger in his
eyes, and a wariness, and knew that this man wanted
something from Nick and was treading a careful path to
get it. It was inconceivable to her that money alone,
even the thousands of dollars at stake, could tempt a
man onto the tightrope Wilson walked.

"Not so formal," he insisted. "Sam. Dani, is it?"
She nodded.

"An unusual name for an unusual lady."

Wilson accepted his drink gratefully when it arrived.
Dani could tell that it was not his first, but he was far

from drunk. He dominated the conversation, making no reference to the reason for the meeting, and Nick let him ramble on about persons in the oil industry, stories about two new discovery wells in Montana, rumors of increased leasing activity in Michigan, commenting only enough to keep Wilson's words flowing, until the wariness faded from his eyes.

Wilson's second drink arrived after a discreet signal from Nick to the waiter. By then the man was comfortable enough to turn his attention to Dani. He refilled her wineglass and gave her the benefit of his practiced smile.

"I haven't seen you around. Have you been in Tulsa long?"

"Not quite five years," she said, willing herself to show no reaction to his visual examination of her. After all, she had assessed him. But his scrutiny was almost a physical assault, and she chafed with the desire to wipe away his egotistical assurance with a scathing retort.

Nick draped his arm over her shoulder, and Wilson's eyes showed that he had noted the act of casual possessiveness. A rueful smile lifted the corners of his mouth for a split second before he returned his attention to Nick.

Why, he thinks I'm Nick's mistress, Dani realized angrily, but as Nick's fingers traced lazy circles on her arm, her anger dissipated and she began to wonder how it would be if she really were what Wilson thought she was. She turned to face Nick and found him looking at her, green lights again dancing in the depths of his eyes and a contented smile magically enhancing his already striking features.

"I think it's time we get down to business," Nick said slowly, "before we forget why we're here."

"You've reconsidered the title opinion then," Wilson asked complacently, "in light of what we discussed yesterday?"

"Yes, I have," Nick told him. "And I'm now even more firmly convinced that the Anderson and Simmons leases aren't worth the paper they're written on."

"They own the minerals," Wilson said, "and neither one has been leased for the last five years."

"And they also both have previous leases to Mid-South, which are still held by production in the adjoining section."

Dani watched quietly as the two men discussed this portion of the conflict. Nick was on familiar territory and could have countered much more strenuous argument than the hackneyed and half-hearted one Wilson put forth before finally letting Nick convince him that the leases were invalid. It seemed to her that Wilson had expected to lose this part and that he was not really upset by it.

Wilson ordered another drink and again filled her wineglass. "So," he said, leaning back in his chair with a sigh. "Even if the Anderson and Simmons interests are held by production, that doesn't affect the leases on the balance."

"Which will expire in three months unless drilling is started before then," Nick reminded him. "Dani, do you have Sam's copy of our proposal?"

Silently she fished the envelope from her purse and handed it to Nick, who passed it across the table. Wilson unfolded the single sheet of paper it contained and scanned it quickly. When he looked up from it, the

wariness was again in his eyes, along with a bitterness
Dani thought must have come from an unanticipated
defeat.

"You intend to hold my feet to the fire on this, don't
you?" Wilson asked in a clipped, strained voice.

"Not at all," Nick told him. "It seems to me that
this is a logical solution to our problem. If you can arrange for Mid-South to farm out their interest in these
leases to me, I'll pick up the entire package."

"Which means that I absorb any additional cost. You
know they're going to want an override."

"The override—" Dani interjected.

"An override," Wilson snapped at her impatiently.
"An overriding royalty interest. A percentage of the
gross income of the well. Taken off the top, along with
the landowner's royalty interest payment, before the operator of the well pays any expenses or takes his share."

Dani did not try to hide the chill in her voice. "I
speak the language, Mr. Wilson. What I started to say is
that the override you have retained will be more than
sufficient to cover any demanded by Mid-South."

"And if they decide not to farm their interest out to
me," Nick went on smoothly, "if they can be per-
suaded to participate in the drilling of the well, with me
as operator, I'll take the valid leases, but only those."

"And if I can't arrange either of those alternatives,
you're going to leave me holding the bag, is that it?"
Wilson said tersely.

"I wouldn't have put it that way." A deadly calm
crept into Nick's voice. "You know very well that if I'm
not able to drill within six weeks, I'll lose the rig I have
contracted, and I won't be able to line up another one
before your leases expire."

Dani flinched inwardly at the venom in Wilson's voice. "I think you've just decided you paid too much for these leases and you've latched onto the first excuse you could find to welch on our agreement."

Nick's hand clenched on Dani's arm, and she could feel the anger running through his body. She raised her hand and clasped his, holding it against her arm, while with her other hand she gripped the slender stem of the wineglass.

"I think," she said softly, "and I've waited all evening for you to say something that would change my mind—I think you approached Nick with this package, knowing there was no way he could ever drill it. I think you knew from the beginning that Mid-South held those leases by production. And I think you're aware of a few more problems that we've not yet discussed."

Wilson swiveled around in his chair to examine the source of this unexpected attack. "Just who the hell are you, lady?"

Nick loosened his grip on her arm but left his hand resting in hers. "I told you, Wilson. You just didn't listen. This is my lawyer, the person who first opened up this can of worms. Dani—D. J. Simms."

The man's eyes registered shock for only a moment before he regained his composure and said evenly, "Those are pretty harsh accusations. Just how do you propose to back them up?"

Dani continued in a low voice. "You don't know about the top leases, of course?" He raised his hand as if to deny any knowledge, but she went on. "Leases that take effect the day yours expire, covering all of the good interests you've offered Nick."

"That's not in the abstracts," he said too quickly.

"No. They were only filed in the County Clerk's office the day before yesterday."

"Then how am I supposed to know about them? There is a lot of leasing activity in the area. I'm not surprised that someone has done it, but you can't hold me responsible for it."

"McCauley is the name of the person who took the leases," Dani told him. "S. J. McCauley." She waited for his response, and when none came, she continued. "McCauley has been busy leasing in that county for about six months. Not all of the leases taken have been assigned to someone else, but most of them have been—to Mid-South.

"Who slipped up and put those leases of record, Mr. Wilson? Did someone in your organization become frightened and advance your schedule without telling you about it, or were you so sure that Nick would accept the good leases you became careless?"

"I haven't the slightest idea what you're getting at. Even if McCauley is working for Mid-South, what's that got to do with me?"

"You don't know S. J. McCauley?" Nick asked.

"No. I never heard of the man."

"Woman." Dani felt the ice in her voice. "Sarah Jane McCauley. I believe that is your mother's maiden name."

Wilson sat very still, visibly paler in the dim light of the room. A vein jumped in his throat as he glared at Dani.

Nick broke the silence. "Under the terms of our contract I have to leave the money in escrow for the balance of the thirty days. If you want it, you know how to get it. We have nothing else to discuss." He turned to Dani in pointed dismissal of the man across the table.

"Why?" Dani asked after Wilson left. "Why would he try something like that? It doesn't make any sense."

"Greed is a funny thing. People have done a lot worse for the kind of money we had at stake."

"But, Nick, you would have found out eventually, and Mid-South would have known. Even the money involved is not enough to warrant his risking whatever professional reputation he has for the sake of one paycheck."

"He was probably counting on my not wanting to advertise the fact that someone had played me for a fool," Nick said with a trace of bitterness in his voice.

"That's more important to you than the money, isn't it?" she prompted, knowing the answer even as she asked the question.

"Yes," he admitted. "But since I'm now safe on both counts, we don't have to worry about that anymore." The look in his eyes softened as he smiled at her "Thank you, counselor."

Curiously uncomfortable, Dani tried to shift his attention away from her. "What will you do now?"

He grinned at her. "Find another drilling prospect and go after it, of course."

"In western Oklahoma?"

"Probably," he said. "I still want to play out there."

She had wondered since the day she had been given the file why he had chosen the western part of the state, and now the combination of unaccustomed wine and the appearance of closeness that had existed between her and the man, Nick Sanders, unlocked questions she would never have dared to ask the client,

Nick Sanders. She spoke carefully, knowing she was dangerously close to prying into areas that were really none of her business.

"I don't understand what drives a person time after time to expend the kind of energy and money that are needed to sink a hole in the ground, never knowing if there is going to be oil there. I know that if there is oil, it's financially rewarding.

"That's an understatement, isn't it?" she said, chuckling. "But you don't need the money." She gestured indecisively toward the other two of the Brady Center towers. "And yet you keep on, spending yourself and risking fortunes, in a series of calculated risks." She found herself hopelessly searching for words to continue.

"It's a game, Dani," Nick told her. "For me, anyway. If I want to build an apartment complex, I go through a series of steps. If I want to build a Brady Center, I go through the same series of steps. Sometimes there are surprises, but more often there aren't. The result is that I wind up with an apartment complex or a Brady Center.

"If I want to drill an oil well, I have a different series of steps to follow. I cover my back. I protect myself by having the best geology, the best engineering, the best drilling, and"—he nodded toward her—"the best legal advice I can get, but I never know what's going to be at the bottom of the hole. And if there is oil there, I'm never sure if I'm going to be able to get it out.

"It's a game," he repeated. "The money is just a way of keeping score."

"And you play the game very well," Dani said with some understanding.

"Yes, I do."

"But why did you suddenly decide to change games?" she asked. "What prompted you to learn a still different set of steps, to go all the way across the state, looking for gas, not oil, drilling eight, nine, ten times as deep as you've ever drilled before, taking on a completely different set of problems?"

A smile twitched at his lips and lighted his eyes. "I thought it would be fun."

Fun. The word mocked her. How many times had Rob gently chastised her for leading him into something because she thought it would be fun. She had convinced him that going to law school together would be fun. She had convinced him that painting the bathroom would be fun.

No! Not now! she screamed inwardly as she averted her head and stared without seeing over the lights of Tulsa. She pulled her protective armor around her, blanking all thought from her mind, refusing to remember.

"Dani?" She felt Nick's fingers on her cheek, turning her toward him. She read his puzzlement in the set of his mouth, which conflicted with the gentleness of his question. "Is the thought of doing something just for the fun of it so abhorrent to you?"

She could not maintain eye contact with him and not tell him how abhorrent it had become. She shrugged slightly and reached for her wineglass. "No," she said after she had taken a sip of the wine. "I was lost in another thought for a moment."

Nick continued to watch her, an air of indecision hovering around him, for a time that seemed to her to stretch on for minutes although she knew it could only have been seconds. Finally the stern set of his mouth softened.

"Dance with me?"

Her refusal was automatic, aided by years of rejecting any type of personal contact. "I don't—"

"Don't tell me you don't dance either?" he teased.

She recognized the haunting melody of Cole Porter's "Night and Day" drifting across the room and recognized that for some reason she wanted to dance with him, wanted to have his arms around her, wanted to feel her body moving rhythmically with his to the sensual strains of the music.

"No, I won't tell you that. It's just that I haven't danced for...for quite some time. I'm rusty."

"I'll risk it," he said, still teasing. "And I'll try to stay off your toes."

He was a strong leader, and he was careful of her toes, but Dani managed to stumble once as she held herself rigid in his unfamiliar embrace.

"Relax," he whispered. "No one's judging your performance."

She smiled at him sheepishly, took a deep breath, and willed herself to relax against him as she exhaled.

Why, he can dance, she discovered to her delight as he glided her across the room with only the slightest pressure of his hand on her back. As she moved with the music written for dancing at a time when man and woman danced together, feeling her confidence growing that she could follow him, she let go of her inhibitions and surrendered to the sheer enjoyment of moving with him.

Nick noticed the difference in her and added variation to the basic step. Dani sensed that he was holding

back, unsure of her ability. She sighed and leaned her
head against his shoulder. There was no need to tell
him. For now she was content just to follow his lead.

The band shifted smoothly into a fox trot. Nick led
her carefully into that, but she heard his soft laugh
when he realized there was no need for caution.

"Rusty, are you?" he murmured against her hair.

"A little." A laugh of sheer delight bubbled from
her.

"Let's see just how rusty," he teased as he swung
her around in a complicated variation.

She recognized the beginnings of an uptempo jazz
number and felt a stab of disappointment. This was
where she thought she'd lose him. He was either going
to beg off or expect them to do two solos. He didn't. He
clasped her more firmly and swirled her across the
room in a series of steps that left her slightly breathless.
She caught a glimpse of the two of them in the mirrored wall by the bandstand. *Can that really be me?* she
wondered at the sight of the slender woman moving
gracefully in Nick's arms. But she had little time to
wonder, only to enjoy.

When the music glided into a waltz, she looked up at
Nick and found her own appreciation reflected in his
eyes.

"No one dances like this anymore," she said to him.
"Where did you learn?"

He grinned back at her. "My mother was insistent
that her boys have all the social graces, so every Saturday morning for what seemed like years I was dressed
in a suit and tie and deposited at the local dance studio
where I reluctantly counted steps and bowed to little
girls in ruffled white dresses. I hated it at the time. And

you? Were you one of those little girls in a ruffled dress?"

"No." She laughed. "I was addicted to old movies on television. I wanted to grow up to be Ginger Rogers."

When the waltz was over, they stood together, arms around each other, facing the band and waiting for the next number. The musicians were aware of them. She could see that in the grins they exchanged as they whispered among themselves, but she was not prepared for the challenge they threw out in the form of a Latin American beat.

"Well, Ginger?" Nick asked, holding his hand out to her.

"A tango?"

He nodded solemnly, but even in this dim light she could see that laughter threatened to overcome him. She slipped her hand into his and gave him an exaggerated smile. "Lead on, Mr. Astaire."

After the last dip they collapsed against each other, shaking with laughter, to applause from other patrons of the club.

The band began playing a jitterbug. "I believe they must be sadists," Nick said in a mock whisper. "Later," he called to them over his shoulder as he led her to their table.

She sank gratefully into her chair and drank thirstily from her wineglass. The wine tasted bitter in her mouth. She was slightly dizzy but couldn't tell if it was from the wine or from excitement. "I've had enough of this," she said as she pushed the glass away from her.

Suddenly Nick's presence seemed formidably close.

She was acutely aware of the subtle scent of his after-shave, the remembered feeling of his arms around her and his body against hers.

"It must be getting late," she said and hated the brittle sound of her voice. "I ought to be getting home."

"Oh, no. I finally found a dancing partner to justify all those hours I spent learning. I'm not about to let you get away this early."

His hand rested on hers. Would he notice the scars? How could he help but notice, she realized, and yet he didn't seem to.

A frown creased his forehead. "How long has it been since you danced like this?" he asked her.

How long? "Forever," she whispered. Rob had tried, but not even Rob had had the flair and natural grace of the man seated beside her. Guilt stabbed at her for comparing them. She slipped her hand from Nick's and picked up her wineglass, meaning only to toy with it, but she carried it to her lips and sipped from it while she searched for something to say.

"What is it, Dani?" he asked gently. "Why do you close yourself off that way?"

"I'm afraid our friend Mr. Wilson and I have some-thing in common," she said, grabbing for the first thing that came to mind and realizing as Nick's face darkened into a scowl that she had said something terri-bly wrong. "I—I just meant," she stammered, "I just meant that I'm a little out of my league."

Nick gazed at her, letting his expression soften, searching her eyes. "I've known you less than a day, but I seriously doubt if there's any situation in which you would be out of your league."

He captured her hand. "You're beautiful, and bright,

and," he said as he pulled her to her feet, "you dance like a dream. Come on," he whispered. "Can't you hear the music calling us?"

She was lost in her own sensations. At some point she slid her right hand from his shoulder to the back of his neck. He held her other hand to his chest. The band, as though in tune with their desires, played only slow, romantic melodies. Their bodies melded together and they moved as one across the floor until the music stopped, silenced for the night.

In a dreamlike trance she walked with Nick to the car. Too soon they were at her apartment, standing in front of the door. She fumbled for her key, not knowing how to say good night to him.

"Dani?" He caught her face in his hands, his fingers trailing along her throat.

"Coffee?" she whispered, knowing only that she didn't want him to leave. Not yet.

Silently, he took the key from her and opened the door, standing to one side to let her enter first.

She crossed the dimly lighted living area to the small kitchen, tossing her purse on the breakfast bar as she passed, not bothering to turn on any other light. She couldn't seem to make her hands obey as she reached for the coffeepot and coffee.

She felt Nick behind her, the warmth of his body burning through her clothes, felt his hands moving on her arms as he pulled her back against him. Part of her wanted to turn and throw her arms around him. The other part strained away from him, trying to measure out coffee with a shaking hand.

"I never did feed you tonight," he whispered against her ear.

"Not food." She too was incapable of anything but a whisper. "But something I needed much more."

The coffee measure dropped into the sink.

"Forget the coffee," he muttered as he turned her toward him.

She stared up at him, warring with the warmth she felt that wanted to answer the desire she saw in his eyes and a cold, hard core within her that hissed insidiously that she had no right to feel this pleasure.

"Nick"—her voice was a broken plea—"I don't..."

"I know," he said, before his mouth silenced her.

For long moments she held herself passive in his arms, refusing to let herself respond as his mouth moved over hers, teasing, tasting, probing, sending rivulets of warmth through her body, but when his hands moved from her arms to her back to enfold her, the battle was lost. Moaning, she strained against him, thrilling to the shudder that ran through him as she twined her fingers in his hair and pulled him closer to her, answering the demand she now felt in his movements with a demand of her own. Years of hunger cried out to be satisfied, and if a voice whispered that only this man had aroused that hunger, the voice was lost in the greater clamor of her need.

Nick drew a ragged breath and pulled away from her, but he didn't seem to be able to let go of her any more than she could release him. He folded his arms around her and pressed her head to his chest. She felt his heart pounding as erratically as hers as both of them fought for breath.

She needed his support to stand. It was as though her bones were molten liquid. She was incapable of anything but holding on to him, wanting him. *I'm not dead.*

One lucid thought penetrated her drugged state. She could feel passion. She could respond. A sob caught in her throat. Not since Rob... She closed her eyes and buried her face against Nick's shirt. She couldn't— wouldn't—think about Rob at a time like this, but his image floated through the blackness behind her closed lids, and when she tried to force it away, her son's agonized wail rose in her ears, drowning out the sound of Nick's heartbeat.

I can't go through that tonight, she thought as panic destroyed her euphoria. *I won't!* She opened her eyes so that the light would erase the pictures and saw Nick looking down at her, his eyes glazed by the same passion she had felt. She didn't have to go through it, she realized. She could lose herself with Nick.

She twisted in his arms and caught his face in her hands. "Nick," she whispered hoarsely, "stay with me tonight."

The barest flicker of surprise showed in his eyes before he bent his head to hers. "Lady," he murmured, "I have no intention of leaving."

Chapter Three

Light from the living room lamp crept through the doorway, casting a warm glow on a sliver of the bedroom. The rest of the room remained lost in darkness. Dani threw back the bed covers and turned hesitantly to face Nick. He had already shed his jacket and tie and stood only inches in front of her, a looming shadow except for the luminescence of the white shirt stretched across his broad chest and shoulders.

A lump caught in her throat and she swallowed, trying in vain to ease the constriction. Self-consciously, but protected by the darkness, she nibbled on her lower lip, unsure of what he expected her to do next.

She plucked at the button of a cuff of her shirt, but he caught her hands in his, unbuttoned the cuffs, and feathered a kiss on the inside of each of her wrists. There was the briefest of pauses before he unbuttoned his own cuffs.

She stood rigidly still as she felt his fingers brush across her breasts and begin unfastening the row of covered buttons down the front of her shirt.

"Help me, Dani," he urged in a low voice.

When she finally understood what he was asking,

she raised shaking hands to the front of his shirt, duplicating his tantalizing movements. His hands crept to her shoulders, easing the silk from her until it slithered to the floor. He stood motionless, waiting. Tremulously, she pushed at his shirt until she freed it from his shoulders and it fell to join hers.

"Oh, Dani, Dani," he murmured as he drew her to him. Beneath her cheek was the springiness of the dark hair that veed down from his throat; beneath her fingers, supple skin that covered coiled muscles.

She felt his hands moving over her, sliding from the satiny second skin of her chemise to the bareness of her flesh. A shudder ran through her, and she clutched at his shoulders. His low laugh told her that he had misread her response, and he continued his exploration, teasing at her until he bent her backward and began exploring with his mouth areas that his hands had already mapped and memorized.

She stood with her body arched against him and her head thrown back and waited, but after the initial shock of his touch she felt...nothing. Oh, God, what was wrong with her? A moment ago she had been a mass of exposed nerves and now, while she was being expertly made love to, the strongest word she could think of to describe what was happening was—pleasurable. Where was the passion? She could still feel it. That had been proven tonight. She would feel it again. She would make herself feel it again!

She began her own exploration of his body, tentatively at first but growing more demanding with an urgency born of her fear, and when his mouth returned to hers she met it with a desperation that translated itself into at least the appearance of desire.

She tensed as she felt his hand on her waistband, but in one fluid motion he sent her skirt and slip to join their shirts. She felt the next move should be hers. Her hands shook so badly though, she abandoned her futile efforts at his belt.

"I . . . I . . ." She had to tell him something but had no idea what she was trying to say.

"Ssh. It's all right," he murmured as he slipped the chemise from her and eased her onto the bed. His touch should have been driving her wild. She knew that. If she were a normal woman, the lingering caress as he drew her hose from her would have had her writhing in anticipation. Instead, she very plainly heard the sound of her shoes being dropped on the floor at the foot of the bed.

What have I gotten myself into? she wondered as Nick turned to divest himself of the rest of his clothing. He stood outlined in the light from the living room. And what had she done to Nick? He deserved more than the shell she had become. She closed her eyes against the sight of his strong, lean body. If she could only go back to the time in the kitchen and take back her rashly uttered words, but she couldn't, any more than she could tell him to stop now because she had changed her mind. She had gone too far not to finish what she'd started.

The tremor that started in her hands had spread until now her whole body quivered, stilled only a second by the shock of feeling Nick's flesh along the length of hers as he stretched beside her and reached to take her in his arms.

Don't ever let him learn the truth, she prayed as she

turned to him to begin a pantomime of the act of love. But she trembled too violently, she reacted too hesitantly. He pulled away from her, leaning on one elbow, stroking her hip with his free hand.

"What's the matter?" he asked gently.

If only he hadn't asked, she might have been able to go through with it. But now there was no way. She couldn't lie to him anymore—not with words—not with her body. Choking back a moan, she twisted away from him, curling into a tight ball on the other side of the bed.

He leaned beside her and placed a whisper-soft kiss on her shoulder. "Dani?" His still gentle voice carried a note of insistence. "What's wrong?"

If only she could stop shaking. If only she could disappear magically from the room. If only she never had to face him again.

"I'm ashamed, Nick," she whispered brokenly. "So ashamed. And afraid."

"You aren't ashamed of enjoying your body, are you?" he murmured at her throat. "It's natural to want to take pleasure, to want to give pleasure."

She shrank away from his hand on her arm. "Nick, listen to me! I'm using you." She felt his body stiffen at her words. "Pretending a desire I don't feel. That's why I'm ashamed."

He caught her shoulders and forced her down, pinioning her beneath him, all traces of tenderness gone from his touch and from his voice. "This was an act?" Enough light penetrated the room for her to see the disgust etched in the harsh lines of his face. "I don't believe you," he groaned.

She twisted helplessly as his head bent to hers, but she endured the punishing ravishment of his mouth and hands without fighting. She deserved much worse.

"Damn you, Dani," he said thickly. "Why?"

She turned her head to one side and closed her eyes. She had to force her words around the constriction in her throat. "Hate me if you have to," she whispered. "Use me if it will help, but I don't feel anything, Nick. Not anything." Her last words were barely audible. "And that's why I'm afraid."

Nick slumped against her. She could not stop her trembling. Even with the warmth of his body covering her, she was cold, so cold. Maybe she was turning to ice, freezing solid to match the frozen lump that once had been her heart. But that didn't excuse what she'd done tonight.

She touched Nick's arm. This time he flinched.

"I'm sorry." She choked out the words. "So very sorry."

"So am I," he said. He pulled himself to one side and looked down at her. "You really didn't feel anything?" he asked as though he still couldn't believe her.

"No." She twisted her head in denial as she spoke. "No, that's not true either." she forced herself to admit. "Earlier—earlier I didn't have to pretend."

Nick traced his fingers along her cheek, and she felt the moisture of tears she could not have shed. When he drew away from her she knew he was leaving, and knowing that she had driven him away didn't ease the ache that cut its way through her weakened defenses. But he moved only to the foot of the bed to retrieve the fallen covers and pull them over the two of them.

"You're freezing," he said as he wrapped her in his arms. He took a deep breath and exhaled slowly before speaking in a voice tight with control. "I'm trying hard to hear what you're actually saying. You told me a number of things tonight that I chose to disregard. You told me that you didn't drink, and I insisted that you do it anyway. You told me that you didn't dance, and I dragged you onto the floor. You even tried, I think, to tell me that you don't take strange men to bed with you, but I didn't let you finish the sentence."

He pulled the covers more securely around her. "The only thing I chose to hear you say tonight was, 'Stay with me,' and that's because I'd done everything I could think of to make sure you said it.

"Dani, will you stop trembling?" His hands moved over her back and arms, not with passion but to knead warmth into her chilled flesh. "What I'm saying is, I think you're trying to take all the blame for what happened when what you probably ought to do is scream at me and tell me to get the hell out of your life."

She murmured an inarticulate sound in her throat. She didn't know what it meant. All she knew was that Nick's warmth was driving the ice away, and she crept closer to him, needing his warmth, needing the protection that, for now, his arms offered.

Dani awoke with a stabbing pain behind her eyes and groaned against the injustice of having to crawl out of the cocoon of bedcovers, but crawl she did, fighting free of the blanket and spread until she sat upright, her head cradled in her hands.

Unable to avoid facing the truth any longer, she peered through her fingers at the disarray of the room.

More than any other thing, the crumpled pillow beside her gave mute testimony of the previous night.

"Oh, no," she moaned, shaking her head. Movement aggravated her headache, but she scrambled from the bed, snatched her pale blue satin robe from the closet, and wrapped it around her.

She stumbled into the living room. The saucer Nick had used for an ashtray still sat on the coffee table. She carried the saucer to the kitchen, dumped its contents, and reached for the coffeepot. Pot and coffee still stood on the drainboard. The measure sat atop an island of grounds in the sink.

Dani clutched the drainboard with both hands. "I didn't do that," she cried. "I didn't!"

She roused herself, cleaned the mess from the sink, and started the coffee. Ravenously hungry, yet revolted by the thought of food, she poured herself a glass of milk and stepped outside. The kitten attacked her bare toes as she knelt down for the newspaper. She pulled him from her and scolded him gently. "I told you to go away. Why do you keep coming back?"

Mewing pitifully, the kitten climbed onto her lap, pawing for the glass of milk in her other hand.

"See, if you'd gone and found a home like I told you to, you wouldn't be hungry this morning," she said gently as she put the kitten from her and picked up her newspaper.

She had to nudge the kitten away from the door with her toe. Why didn't he go away? He had been there a week, greeting her every morning. And he did look hungry. No. If she fed him once, he would never go away. And yet, she could still hear his mewing outside the door.

Muttering an oath, she snatched a small bowl from the cabinet and carried it outside. "Just don't come to depend upon this," she snapped as she poured half her milk into the bowl. The kitten didn't appear to hear her. He was too busy attacking the milk.

Dani spread the newspaper out on the breakfast bar and stared at the front page, unable to focus her attention on any story, while she waited for the coffee to finish brewing. Her mind kept wandering back to one subject—Nick Sanders. Finally she stopped fighting it and let herself think about him and then wished she hadn't because what she remembered most clearly was the look of disgust on his face when she told him she couldn't—she couldn't— She crossed her arms on the breakfast bar and lay her head on them while waves of shame washed through her. At least, she assured herself, she'd never have to see him again.

The shrill of the telephone jolted her upright, but it was not until the second ring that she identified the sound. She hurried to the desk to avoid hearing the shriek a third time.

"D.J.?" she heard Marcie ask hesitantly.

"Yes, Marcie. What is it?"

"Are you all right? Your voice sounds strange."

Dani tried to clear the cobwebs from her brain and the cotton from her mouth. "I'm fine," she said clearly. "Is something wrong?"

"No." The woman's voice was puzzled. "It's just that it's almost ten and—"

"Ten?" Dani yelped.

"Yes. And it's not like you to be this late without checking in. I was afraid something might have happened."

Dani pulled out the desk chair and slipped onto it, propping an elbow on the desk and resting her head against her hand. "I overslept. I'm just now getting around."

"The meeting with Sam Wilson must have been a tough one."

Dani didn't want to be reminded. "You might say that. What have I missed so far this morning?"

"Nothing critical, I think. Mr. Merriweather wants to see you at two. You don't have anything else scheduled at that time."

"Would you call his secretary and tell her I'll be there?"

"Sure. The abstracts have arrived for the Win-Tech drilling opinion."

"Fine."

"And Nick Sanders called."

Dani felt the blood draining from her face. She gripped the receiver, but her voice was calm when she spoke. "Did he leave a message?"

"No. He said he'd call back later. But the reason I called is that this is the day I have the doctor's appointment."

Dani only half heard the her.

"I have to be there by eleven, D.J., and I may be a little late getting back from lunch. I can reschedule the appointment if I have to, but I'd really rather not."

"No," Dani told her. "I'll call Chet and ask him to send someone in."

"Thanks, D.J. It is important or I wouldn't have asked. What do you want me to tell Mr. Sanders when he calls back? That you're at home and he can reach you there for a while?"

"No!" Dani said quickly. "Tell him that I"—she chose her words carefully, not wanting to ask Marcie to tell an outright lie—"tell him that I said I had a number of things to take care of outside the office today and probably won't be in."

"Oh." Marcie's one syllable spoke volumes.

Nick had called. Dani pushed that thought aside as she punched out the numbers for her office, grateful for this small activity, and asked to be connected with Chet Davis. He answered the phone himself, sounding preoccupied and impatient, and well he should be, she thought. As office manager, he was responsible for everything from the personnel records and payroll for thirty-five attorneys and a greater number of support personnel to making sure that paper clips and staples were ordered regularly.

"You'd think," Dani said dryly, "that the man in charge of hiring could manage to find a secretary for himself."

Because this was a running joke in the office, nurtured primarily by his good-humored complaints, Chet laughed.

"Good morning, D.J.," he said pleasantly. "You'll be happy to know that I have found someone. I'm transferring Robin up from word processing, but I can't bust her loose from that job until Monday. What can I do for you today?"

"I won't be in until after lunch, and Marcie has an appointment. Could you float someone over to cover her telephone for a couple of hours?"

"Sure. If you don't mind her doing someone else's typing while she's there."

"Any way you can work it out will be all right with me," she told him.

"Speaking of working something out, if you're at the courthouse, would you mind doing me a favor?"

"I'm sorry, Chet. As a matter-of-fact, I haven't left the house yet."

"Oh, well. It was worth a try." His voice softened. "You're not sick or anything, are you?"

She hated the note of solicitude she heard. When they first met, he had tried to hide his concern, sensing, correctly, that she would reject it. Now, after all this time, it had crept back into his voice. "No, Chet," she said grimly. "I'm fine."

She replaced the receiver and glanced blindly around the room. "Just fine," she repeated.

The phone rang one other time that morning, while she huddled in a corner of the couch, nursing a cup of coffee, having consciously blanked all thought from her mind. She jumped at the first shrill demand, but she knew she wouldn't answer it. "Coward," she hissed at herself as she watched the telephone, counting the rings, until it was again silent.

Dani collected her messages from the relief secretary and tackled the stack of abstracts waiting for her. After the first few pages, though, she realized she still couldn't concentrate. About all she was capable of doing, she found, was signing her name to the correspondence Marcie had left on her desk. Eventually she abandoned even that, wandered to the window, and looked down on the busier than usual street.

"D.J.?" Marcie stood in the doorway, smiling radiantly, still wearing her jacket and carrying her purse.

"Oh, hi, Marcie," Dani said listlessly. "Did you get a clean bill of health?"

"Yes, I did." Her smile faded as she looked at Dani. She crossed the room and stood by her side, looking down at the street.

"Why is there so much activity this afternoon?" Dani wondered aloud.

"You don't know?" Marcie asked and then continued softly. "They're dedicating the third Brady Center Tower and the pedestrian walkway this afternoon. There's a nice spread about it in the business section of this morning's paper. Oh, by the way, I gave him your message," she added.

"Thank you," Dani told her, her thanks including the woman's tact in not questioning her.

"You look awful, D.J.," Marcie said, her voice teasingly reproving.

"Thanks a lot."

"If it's any consolation, he didn't look as though he'd gotten much sleep either."

Dani's head jerked up. "Where did you see him?" she asked before she could stop herself.

"The same place half the people in town did." Marcie laughed. "He was the guest on *Tulsa Today* this morning. Of course, I was busy getting Joe off to work so I couldn't just sit and watch. You know, you ought to go home and go to bed, but you won't." Marcie fished a bottle of aspirin from her purse. "So why don't you take a couple of these and close your eyes for a few minutes. I'll rouse you in plenty of time to be ready for your appointment with Mr. Merriweather."

Dani took the aspirin and leaned back in her chair, but she didn't sleep. With pain-glazed eyes she stared at the trio of towers, wishing somehow she could relive the past twenty-four hours.

Dani did not look forward to her appointment with Frank Merriweather. At sixty, he exuded, if possible, even more charismatic charm than he had at thirty, when he won his first landmark case in an appeal to the United States Supreme Court. Founder of the firm of Merriweather, Pratt, Widlyme and Tanner, he was the force behind its phenomenal growth. He set the standard of excellence each of the staff attorneys was expected to meet. His hair was completely silver now, and his features had thickened slightly over the years, but he could still dazzle a jury or lull an adversary with consumate skill.

Dani was still somewhat in awe of this man, although she had known him for almost five years. His keen gray eyes missed little, and she dreaded subjecting herself to their examination in her present frame of mind.

His secretary was not at her desk when Dani arrived. She tapped on the open door to his private office and, at a gesture from him, entered and seated herself in one of a pair of deep leather chairs. She waited quietly for him to finish a telephone conversation.

He replaced the receiver and smiled at her. "Nick Sanders called me this morning."

She steeled herself to show no outward reaction, but—damn the man! How long would she have to endure having him thrown at her everywhere she turned?

Mr. Merriweather went on without a pause. "He was pleased with the way you handled the Wilson matter. He said you had a 'unique blend of intuition and hardheaded common sense.'"

Frank Merriweather could have no idea of the irony those words conveyed to Dani, and she certainly wasn't going to enlighten him.

"I've known that for some time, D.J.," he continued, "but its gratifying to have a client of Nick's stature confirm my opinion."

"It was kind of him to mention it to you," she murmured.

"Kind is hardly the word I would have chosen." He smiled as he spoke. "Nick expects quality work from this firm. That's why we've managed to keep him as a client for twelve years. He isn't lavish with praise, but occasionally he does commend someone for exceptional work. From what he told me about Wilson, I believe he was only being fair in commending you."

"Thank you," she said simply.

"You're a definite asset for this firm, and I appreciate that."

She didn't want to refer to it, but she knew that she had to. "I'm glad. I never want you to regret the chance you took when you hired me."

"D.J., listen to me," he said sternly. "Any chance I took was minimal, and it was years ago. You've made your own way since then. You've earned each advancement, and you've more than repaid any debt you might feel you owe me. I don't even think about it unless you remind me. It's time to put that behind you."

"I know," she said, studying her intertwined fingers before she looked up at him and attempted to smile. "I really do know that."

"Are you all right?" he asked in a softer voice.

She nodded without speaking.

"You look tired today. Are we working you too hard?"

"No!" Dani denied vehemently. "I love my work, Mr. Merriweather."

"You may love it, but you can't go on forever eating, sleeping, and breathing the law. Don't you think it's time you started building a life for yourself that doesn't revolve around this office?"

For once Dani didn't try to hide the pain she felt. There was no need. This man knew most of her secrets. "I don't know if I can."

Chapter Four

When Dani finally convinced herself that she would get nothing accomplished at the office that afternoon, she loaded files and a portable dictation unit into her briefcase, telling herself that later that evening she would be able to concentrate.

Even mundane chores such as picking up the laundry and dry cleaning and shopping for the few groceries she needed proved almost too much for her. After standing in the supermarket weighing a head of lettuce in each hand for untold moments, she tossed both back into the produce bin in disgust and grabbed up only necessary items, which by now included a package of aspirin.

The dim coolness of her apartment did not welcome her. Although she had carefully removed all traces of Nick's visit, his presence lingered, taunting her.

She put away laundry and groceries and fixed herself a sandwich, but after a few bites her stomach revolted, and the sandwich, like the lunch she had prepared, wound up feeding the garbage disposal instead of her.

She swallowed two of the aspirins and filled the bathtub with steaming water, thinking to soak away the mass of aches that filled her, but in the solitude of the tub she heard Nick's voice teasing, "I seriously doubt if there's any situation in which you would be out of your league." Well, he knew now he was wrong. She bit back a moan. But he didn't know just how wrong he had been.

Furious with herself, she scrubbed viciously and toweled dry with the same lack of gentleness. She threw on the long satin and lace nightgown that matched her pale blue robe, put on her slippers, and cinched the robe around her. She caught sight of her reflection in the mirror as she subjected her hair to merciless brushing. She stopped the brush in its descent, holding it poised and ready for another stroke.

"I don't have to do this," she told her reflection as she dropped the brush. There was an escape the doctors had given her those first months and had never taken away from her. She pulled open a drawer in the vanity and found the prescription bottle. One pill, twelve hours of oblivion, and this whole thing would be no more than one of her dreams. Less, she corrected herself. Much less. Because Nick Sanders really meant nothing to her.

"No!" she cried, flinging the bottle down and slamming the drawer. "I can't go crawling back to those. I've come too far."

She stared at the hollow-eyed reflection facing her, at the wide blue eyes that until now had managed not to show the pain she carried with her constantly. She raised her fingers to her face and traced along her cheek. "Did I really cry?" she asked, and the wonder she felt carried into her voice. She leaned her head against the mirror. "Maybe there's hope for me yet."

Once calmed she found that she could concentrate enough to tackle the work she'd brought home with her. She started with routine things first, but half a pot of coffee later she was well on her way to finishing the work she'd assigned herself.

So engrossed in work was she that when the knock sounded on the door her pen slid across the page, leaving a trail of ink. A quick glance at the clock confirmed that it was almost nine, and she certainly wasn't expecting company.

She inched the door open, holding most of her weight behind it, and her heart seemed to somersault into her throat. Standing on her sidewalk, tie askew, shirt sleeves rolled up to his elbows, juggling two sacks and a large, flat box in one arm, stood the man she had been trying, all day, to forget.

A wary smile didn't quite soften Nick's harsh features.

"I've brought the supper I didn't feed you last night."

She stood speechless.

"I got away as early as I could."

Dimly, it registered that there must have been festivities scheduled in connection with the dedication.

"Have you eaten yet?" he asked when she remained silent.

Dani found her voice. "I tried."

"Are you going to let me in?" he asked.

She opened the door and stepped back, her heart pounding furiously, and he crossed the room, cleared a place on the low coffee table, and began pulling food from the sacks.

"A little queasy today, were you?" He grinned at her.

She nodded her head, still not speaking, still not moving from her place by the door, too conscious of the flimsy lace and satin she wore.

"I thought you might be. What you need," he told her, tearing open the second sack, "is Mama Giuseppina's deep pan pizza."

He laughed outright at the look of disbelief she knew was on her face.

"Trust me," he said. "Spicy food will help." He reached into the first sack and took out two large plastic cups. "Iced tea," he said before reaching back into the sack. "But if you can bring yourself to touch it, a little of Mama's homemade wine will help settle the butterflies.

"What are you doing, just standing there?" he asked when she made no response. "We need small plates for the pizza, forks for the salad, and glasses."

He might as well have snapped his fingers, she thought, as she watched him from the safety of the doorway. How could he come back into her life and just . . . take over, ordering her about as though nothing had happened? But she moved reflexively toward the kitchen, seeing herself as she went, knowing she was going, and not having the slightest idea why she was doing what he told her to.

When she returned from the kitchen with the necessary utensils, Nick had pulled the table away from the couch. He sat on the floor, his long legs crossed beneath him and his back resting against the sofa. He patted the floor beside him and, after a pause, she joined him.

He lifted a slice of pizza onto her plate and pushed a container of salad toward her. "Eat," he said before filling his plate.

Dani knew there was no way her stomach could tolerate the rich food, but an unexpected shyness kept her from protesting. It would be easier to nibble at the food than argue why she shouldn't, so hesitantly, she sampled a little. To her surprise, she found he was right. The combination of tangy salad dressing, spicy pizza, and homemade wine did settle the queasiness.

Nick kept up a steady stream of chatter, making no reference to the night before, and soon she found her shyness disappearing.

"What does the 'J' stand for?" he asked as she reached for more pizza.

"What?"

"The 'J' in D.J. What does it stand for?"

She glanced at him out of the corner of her eye.

"That bad?" he asked, laughing.

His laughter was infectious. "No, it's not that bad." She grinned back at him. "But I swear, if you laugh, I'll throw you out of here bodily. Promise not to laugh?"

He nodded solemnly.

"It's Juliet," she murmured.

"It's what?"

"Juliet!" she snapped, but her own laughter softened her voice.

"Danielle Juliet Simms?" He shook his head, but he didn't laugh. "Your mother must have been an incurable romantic."

"I wouldn't know," Dani said, focusing her attention on the now almost insurmountable task of cutting into her pizza. "I never met the woman."

Nick's hand closed over hers. "Dani, I'm sorry."

She saw genuine concern in his eyes. "Don't be," she said softly. "I had to come to grips with that a long time ago. I've done all right without her; probably better than I would have if she'd kept me around as a reminder of an indiscretion she'd just as soon forget.''

From long years of practice, Dani knew how to shift the conversation to safer topics. "You must feel like king of the mountain after having had so much attention today," she teased. "Did you have a good time?"

"I'm not supposed to admit something like that," he said, taking her lead and reverting to his earlier, easier attitude.

"I'm supposed to proclaim to all who will listen that I was bored beyond belief, but the truth is I would have loved every minute of it, if it hadn't started so early and lasted so late."

With her quiet prompting he kept them laughing with stories about the day's adventures, and misadventures, until the last crumb disappeared from the take-out tray. He offered to refill her glass with wine, but she shook her head, reached instead for the iced tea, and leaned back against the sofa.

"Thank you for the meal," she said, sighing contentedly. "I think I was starving."

He slanted sideways beside her, resting his elbow on the couch near her head. "From the way you attacked the pizza, a person would think you hadn't eaten anything in a couple of days."

"That's about right," she murmured. "I couldn't tolerate anything today, and yesterday I was so busy I didn't take time for anything but an apple."

"No wonder you..." Whatever he started to say broke off in his delighted laugh. He dropped his hand to her head and ruffled her hair. "You really don't drink, do you?"

She was suddenly, acutely aware of him. When she turned to face him, his green eyes no longer laughed. He lifted his hand from her hair.

"Very little," she said, wanting to look away from him and yet unable to move. "And not for a long time."

Nick broke the spell. He stuffed the trash into the remaining sack, stacked the dishes, and carried them to the kitchen.

When he returned, he held his hand out to her, looking into her eyes, compelling her to reach out to him. Dani couldn't find the strength to disobey. She slipped her hand into his, and he pulled her to her feet and into his arms, molding her to him.

"You're even smaller than I remembered."

"Nick, I—"

He ignored her protests. "This is ridiculous," he said. "I can't kiss you the way I want without breaking your back." He gripped her by the waist, but the satin slipped and his hands grazed her breasts before coming to rest under her arms as he lifted her onto the coffee table.

"Nick, I..." Dani fought the panic clawing at her throat as Nick's hands moved down her back, pressing her to him. "I can't do this!" she cried. "My God, do you know what it would do to me to have to live through another scene like last night?"

He pulled away only enough to be able to look into her eyes. "I don't think I'd get through it again very well myself."

Embarrassment held her still as she recognized the restraint behind his words.

"I'm sorry," she whispered.

"Relax," he told her gently. "I'm only going to kiss you good night, and then you are going to walk me to the door and lock it behind me."

He didn't give her time to refuse. His lips touched hers in what started as a gentle salute and deepened into a questioning probe of her senses. Dani's lips parted beneath his as, unbelievably, she felt warmth flooding through her body. She dug her fingers into his shoulders and sighed against him as they clung together, tasting each other, for fragile precious minutes, until he pulled away.

"Oh, Dani," he moaned, and she saw his need written in his eyes.

She touched his cheek in mute sympathy. "Why did you come back?"

He managed a lopsided grin. "Damned if I know. And you? Why didn't you slam the door in my face when I did?"

With her mind reeling as it was, there was no way she could find an answer. Besides, he had already said it so well. She tried to smile. "Damned if I know either."

"There's a guest pianist with the Philharmonic tomorrow night," he said abruptly.

She tried to follow the jump in thought but gave up. "I know," she said, bewildered.

"I know you know." He lifted her from the table and stood her carefully on the floor several inches in front of him. "Wear your russet silk. It matches the highlights in your hair."

"How do you know about that dress?" she stammered.

He was back on easy footing now, smiling broadly. "Today I was called a, quote, intrepid visionary—"

"That's awful." Laughter bubbled from her. "Simply awful."

"I know," he admitted, "but as one, whatever one is, I feel I am entitled to a few visionary secrets. Oh, yes. Tomorrow night you will not sit alone. I will pick you up and escort you. In case you didn't recognize it," he added, "that's the intrepid part."

"Did anyone dare to call you an idiot?" she chided.

"No. That's a term I reserve for my personal use."

Dani dressed with special care the following evening, feeling curiously inept as she did so. "Stop acting like a lovesick schoolgirl," she scolded, because she felt that was how she was acting, but if she hadn't been able to stop herself so far, why should she think she could now? After Nick left the night before, she had turned on the television to watch the late news, knowing that his day's activities would be highlighted. She sat with her knees tucked under her chin and her arms wrapped around her legs, watching enthralled as he moved so confidently among the dignitaries gathered for the occasion, listening to his voice as he explained his plans for renovation of other property in North Tulsa and reiterated that no structurally sound buildings of historic significance had been destroyed for the Brady Center. But she saw all the time the glow in his eyes as he had said good night, and she heard along with the televised sound his voice saying, "Damned if I know." She had retrieved the business section of the newspaper from the trash, and even now it rested beneath lingerie in her dresser.

She slipped on the russet silk, smoothing its long folds and studying it with fresh appreciation. It was a deceptive dress, appearing demurely prim on the hanger. On her, though, it was anything but prim. She had bought it on a rare impulse and had worn it only once, to an opening night performance of the Tulsa Theater League, before deciding that it was much too seductive to be worn by an unescorted woman who wanted to remain unescorted.

But Nick had requested— No, Nick had commanded that she wear this, and she was glad that he had. But how had he known about it? She felt a blush rising as she realized he must have seen it in her closet that first night. So much for his visionary status. He was right, though. With her hair coiled, she hadn't noticed, but with it hanging loose she could see that its burnished highlights matched the color of the dress.

She draped the dress's matching fringed shawl over her arms and walked into the bedroom to examine herself in the full-length mirror. A frown puckered her brow as she wondered, momentarily, about her motives for being so pleased with her appearance, but she didn't have time to wonder long, because she heard footsteps on the sidewalk outside, followed by a purposeful knock on her door.

She was prepared for his striking good looks this time, but still the sight of him in the black suit the occasion demanded and the white-on-white silk shirt with gold cuff links did strange things to the pit of her stomach. She clutched the doorknob as she opened the door and stepped back for him to enter.

"Lovely," he said as he met her look with an equally intense one of his own. "Are you ready?"

"Almost."

Dani caught a whiff of the subtle scent of his after-shave lotion as he walked past her into the room. She swallowed. Suddenly she was not at all sure that going out with him again was a good idea. "I just have to finish changing purses," she said as she closed the outer door and hurried into the bedroom.

She threw the few necessary items into her evening bag—lingering over the task would give her too much time to think—and returned to the living room in less than a minute. Nick sat on the couch, leaning over the coffee table, his slender, capable fingers idly tracing the rim of the oversized alabaster ashtray she had purchased that afternoon.

"I was running out of dishes," she said a little defensively.

"I'd feel singularly honored," he said as he smiled up at her, "if I hadn't seen the new dish you bought for your cat on the front porch."

"He's not my cat," Dani insisted. "He just won't go away."

"So you're feeding him to make him leave? Are you that bad a cook?"

Dani felt the laughter growing within her as she watched a mischievous smile play across Nick's features. It was going to be all right. This evening was going to be all right.

"Don't forget your ticket," he reminded her as they started out the door. She snatched it off the desk, puzzled about why she would need it, unless he planned not to sit with her, and that didn't seem at all in character. However, once they arrived at the Performing Arts Center, she understood why he'd asked her to bring it. There was a long line of students in front of the box office.

Nick paused at one side of the lobby instead of leading her directly inside. "It's what I usually do with my extra ticket," he told her. "Which one do you think is most in need of a free dose of Rachmaninoff?"

Dani studied the line. A number of students were obviously together. One isolated seat wouldn't help them. Nor would it help a young couple who stood arm in arm. She finally decided on a painfully thin young man in sneakers, frayed jeans, and a Windbreaker.

"Do you want to take it to him?" Nick asked.

"Oh, no," Dani said in dismay. "I'm afraid I might come off like Lady Bountiful, and that wouldn't do at all."

Nick took the ticket to the boy, and the two of them exchanged a few words before breaking into laughter. The young man smiled broadly at her as he accepted the ticket.

"You made a good choice," Nick told her as they waited to be seated. "He's a piano major."

"What did you tell him?" Dani asked, remembering the laughter.

"Never mind." His lips twitched as he glanced down at her.

The usher came for them then, and she was forced to be silent until after they were seated.

"What did you tell him?" she insisted.

He leaned toward her and whispered against her ear. "I told him that you were threatening to use your own ticket, and that I couldn't bear to be parted from you. I asked him to do me a favor by removing any possibility you would escape from me."

She shot him a mock grimace. "But how did you know I had the ticket?"

Nick gestured with his program. "There's our studious young friend," he pointed out. "You always sit in that seat. That indicates a season ticket."

She *always* sat in that seat? Never mind that she did always sit in that seat, but how did he know? She turned in the seat to face him and found him looking maddeningly secretive. "But I haven't worn this dress to a symphony performance."

"Remember my mother's insistence on acquiring social graces?" he asked.

"Yes?"

"Some of it took." He grinned openly now. "I recognized you in the hallway at your office. I just didn't know who you were except the woman I'd seen at the symphony, the theater, and the ballet."

Dani felt vaguely uncomfortable and not at all sure he was being truthful. "Not the opera?" She tempted him with one thing that would tell her he lied.

"I'm afraid I'm not that cultured." He looked at her sharply. "Do you enjoy it?"

Applause greeted the entrance of the conductor. Dani toyed with the thought of not answering Nick but couldn't resist chuckling. "I don't go either."

She leaned back in her chair in anticipation as music filled the room. Soon she was lost to all but the sheer sensory enjoyment of the music playing over her, washing through her, filling an emptiness within her as nothing else ever had. She looked down once, at her hand resting in Nick's. She glanced at him to find he was as lost in the music as she had been. Smiling contentedly, she once again succumbed to the orchestra's magic.

Dani always left the symphony hall in a state of mild

euphoria, but tonight, with Nick at her side, his arm around her as he guided her to the car, the world was not one inch short of perfect.

"Would you like to have dinner now?" he asked as he started the car.

"Not right now," she murmured.

"Then what do you want to do?" he asked softly.

"Would you think I was terribly silly if I said I wanted to walk in the night air and feel the music?"

"Not at all." He pulled smoothly out into the traffic but instead of merging with it on its suburban-bound journey, he turned, circled a few blocks, and pulled up at a parking meter on the outer edge of Main Mall.

"Our private boulevard," he said as he helped her from the car. "There's not another soul in sight."

"It's different at night," Dani mused aloud as they walked, arms entwined, among the plantings in the center of the landscaped pedestrian mall that had been Main Street.

"Without the rush, the press of people having to be somewhere and not wanting to be where they are?" he asked.

"Something like that." She collected a stray thought. "How often have you just strolled through here for the sheer enjoyment of it, or to feel the breeze on your face, or to admire this city for the beauty it is?"

"Not often enough," he admitted, "but I have done it."

"I never have," she told him. "Not once in the years I've been here, until tonight. And that saddens me."

They stopped at the fountain that dominated the center of what had once been a busy intersection and stood side by side, his arm over her shoulder, hers around his waist, in the fresh April air. No stars twinkled in the inky sky overhead, but scattered lights in the towers rising on all sides glittered instead. The fountain created its own music, and occasional droplets of water, caught by the gentle breeze, kissed their faces.

"It is a magical night," she said, sighing as she rested her head against him.

His arm tightened cautiously on hers. "I want to hold you, Dani."

Her breath caught, and her heart seemed to stop in midbeat. "I want you to hold me, Nick," she whispered. It tore something within her to say the words, but she knew she had to. "But I'm still afraid."

"I know," he said, breathing deeply as he turned to enfold her in a tentative embrace. "And I don't know what to do about that."

He twined his hand in her hair at the back of her head and pressed her cheek to his chest. "I don't know what's happened to you. I can't begin to understand what happened Wednesday night."

"Nick . . ."

"No. Hush," he murmured. "I'm not asking you to try to explain. Let's do something else." He spoke guardedly, as though having to find words to fit half formed thoughts. "Let's begin again and try to forget Wednesday night ever happened. I promise I won't push you any farther than you want to go, and I won't pry into areas you don't want me to know about. I think we can have something good together, Dani, if we're careful."

Dani shook her head against his chest, wanting to believe that what Nick said was possible but knowing her private hell would never let it happen. "I can't make any promises."

"The only promise I'm asking from you is that you do your best not to close yourself off from me. Can you go that far?"

It sounded like so little when he asked it that way, and yet—she pushed the *and yets* from her mind and leaned against him in surrender. "I'll do my best."

She felt him release pent-up breath, but his arms retained their gentle hold on her as if he, too, recognized the fragility of the moment. They leaned against each other for countless minutes with only the splashing of the fountain and the rare sound of a distant car horn penetrating the silence that enveloped them.

He spoke first. "I don't want to let you go, but if we stand here much longer, I'm going to break one of my new promises."

She laughed a little shakily at the exaggerated regret his voice carried and stepped back from him. He held out his hand to her, and she clasped it. They turned and wandered toward the car, silent until they neared the end of the mall.

"I know a little all-night café in south town," he said in a voice that resembled his normal tone, "where we can get eggs Benedict, if you don't mind sitting at a counter."

"With real hollandaise sauce?" she asked in a voice that resembled hers. "Not a mix?"

"Not a mix."

"I might be willing to sit on the floor for that."

He stopped and pulled her to his side. She waited breathlessly, not knowing what to expect. He bent to her and placed a light kiss on her lips. A satisfied smile danced in his eyes.

"I knew you'd say that."

She felt an answering smile on her face. It was a magical night.

"Can you run in those shoes?" he asked in another of his abrupt shifts.

"I don't know." She felt laughter starting to rise in her again.

He still held her hand. "Well, pick up your skirt and let's find out. I feel like running. Do you feel like running?"

Her laughter bubbled over. "Why not?"

Chapter Five

What followed Dani could only describe as a courtship, an old-fashioned, concentrated courtship. Recognizing it for what it was, she felt a secret surge of pleasure.

Nick had no way of knowing that she had never been courted before. There had been no need for it. She and Rob had grown up together, had known each other since they were twelve and she had been placed in the last of a long line of foster homes, next door to his mother's house. They were fast friends before they started dating, finding with each other a warmth neither had in their homes, sharing everything from sandlot baseball to dreams of a home where love flowed openly. It seemed only natural for them to be with each other through adolescence. By their senior year in high school, each had known that they would spend their lives together, in spite of Rob's mother's disapproval of her background, and in spite of the fact that once Dani reached eighteen her foster parents would willingly relinquish any lingering social responsibility they might once have felt toward raising a needy child.

Dani pushed those thoughts from her mind. That part of her life was over. Completely, irrevocably over.

There was now an excitement in her life that she had never known. With Nick. Whether it was standing in awe before the marvels of nature in a painting by Bierstadt or Moran at the Gilcrease Museum or quietly watching the swans in a small lake nestled only blocks from the heart of downtown, whether it was dining among the glitter of a Las Vegas-type show or grabbing a few moments together for a quick lunch of hot dogs and lemonade on a bench in the Main Mall, Nick was carefully and expertly seducing her back to life.

What guilt she felt in taking Nick's time and attention while knowing there could be nothing between them she rationalized away as best she could. After all, he wasn't asking anything from her in return, and she had told him that she couldn't make any promises. Cold logic told her that soon he would be gone. What could it hurt to take what he offered for just a short while longer?

Dani found herself looking forward to being with him, hearing his voice on the telephone, catching first sight of him moving through the crowds on the sidewalk to join her. Of course, it was just the excitement of being courted that caused the flutter of anticipation she felt when she thought of him, just the strangeness of being catered to that intensified that feeling when she was with him.

Nick's attitude helped to put her at ease. He didn't again mention the horrible ending of their first night together. It was as though it had never happened. When he draped his arm over her shoulder, or they touched, dancing or walking side by side, it seemed so casual, so natural, Dani was almost able to forget. Almost.

When Nick had brought her home after the symphony, he stopped at the doorway, his hands on her shoulders, and for one agonizing moment, she stiffened at his touch. Grinning, he stooped and picked up the purring kitten that had wrapped itself around his ankles.

"Hello, Not Dani's Cat," he said softly. "I hate to tell you this, old boy, but I think we're both out in the cold tonight." He placed the cat in Dani's hands and brushed a kiss across her lips. "See you tomorrow," he whispered.

Since that time, his kisses had been undemanding. He held himself in control, never pushing her to the exquisite torture she had felt with him before, never taking her to the point where her body would chill in rejection.

And why had it? she wondered angrily. Never before had her body played such a cruel trick on her. But then, never before had it been anyone but Rob making her senses sing. And never before had she spent five years suppressing—no, relentlessly stamping out—all traces of any emotion that managed to surface from the thing that had been her heart. And never before, she admitted to herself during a sleepless night, had she ever attempted to use her body, or someone else's, as an antidote for her misery.

Nick was consistently understanding, consistently gentle, but once during the following days she had glimpsed a facet of him that frightened her. She shivered involuntarily whenever she thought of the coldness in his voice and in his eyes. They were leaving a crowded late-night restaurant where they had stopped for pie and coffee, and he paused in the lobby to get a package of cigarettes. As she stood beside the cigarette machine, she glanced over the crowd waiting to be seated. She caught sight of a slender dark-haired man who, even though he stood with his back to her, seemed familiar. As she puzzled over his identity, she happened to look at the woman beside him, a stunning, tall redhead whose mass of hair was drawn tightly away from her face in an intricately styled Grecian knot emphasizing patrician features and flawless skin. Her eyes were her most arresting feature. Brilliant green, they flicked a disdainful dismissal over Dani before concentrating on Nick. Dani held back a gasp at what she saw as undisguised hatred. When Nick straightened from the machine and dropped his hand on her shoulder, she nodded toward the redhead. "Friend of yours?"

She felt his hand clench painfully into her shoulder as his body stiffened and he swore under his breath. "I didn't know she was back in town," he said as he hurried her from the restaurant.

"Who was she, Nick?" Dani asked in the uncomfortable silence of the car.

"Marilyn," he said tightly. "My ex-wife."

"Oh." The word seemed meaningless in the distance between them. Dani stared in confusion at the darkened streets. "She's beautiful," she said in a small voice.

"So it would appear," he answered in clipped tones.

He remained silent as he walked her to her door, took the key from her, and pushed the door open. She hesitated as he handed her the key, knowing he shouldn't come in but not wanting him to leave while what she read as anger still tensed his body.

"Go in the house, Dani," he said coldly.

She put a tentative hand on his arm but made no move to enter the apartment. He stared down at her hand before meeting the question she knew was in her eyes. She knew in that moment that he would not answer it, and her hand tightened on his arm.

"Oh, damn," he moaned as he clutched her to him. He crushed his mouth against hers, and his arms forced the breath from her as he pressed her against him. She endured his violence as his mouth plundered hers, sensing a pain in him that had nothing to do with her.

Abruptly he released her, leaving her leaning limply against the wall for support. "I told you to go in the house," he said raggedly.

She looked into his eyes and saw a glimmer of the pain she had sensed, and something else. Was that regret reflected in their green depths? Whatever it was, she knew that she couldn't let him leave with the anger he still felt.

With one slender finger she traced the line of his jaw.

"Not this way," she whispered. She caught his face between her hands, holding him still, stretched upward and placed her lips on his, moving gently, tenderly against his mouth. A shudder ran through him before he folded his arms around her and his mouth softened against hers, returning her tenderness.

With a deep sigh she pulled away from him and then leaned against him, leaving her hands resting on his chest as she listened to the thud of his heart beneath her cheek.

"Now," she said with only a slight quaver in her voice, "I think I'd better go in the house."

He held onto her arms as he pulled away from her and studied her face. "See you tomorrow?" he asked.

Wishing with all her heart that she had the courage to ask him to stay with her now, she hesitated before answering, and his hands tightened on her arms. Words deserted her. She managed to smile at him and to nod her head in agreement. He didn't return the smile, but he did brush a kiss across her forehead before turning her and pushing her toward the open door.

"If I didn't know you better, D.J.," Marcie said as she entered Dani's office and caught her absently staring out the window while the melody of Cole Porter's "Night and Day" whispered through her mind, "I'd say I was looking at a woman who's falling in love."

Dani snapped out of her reverie and jerked upright in her chair. "Don't be ridiculous, Marcie. Just because I've gone out with a man a few times, it doesn't necessarily mean—" She broke off when she saw Marcie's broad grin. "I am acting kind of silly, aren't I? Staring out the window and jumping when the phone rings. It's just that it's been so long since I had any kind of life outside this office."

"Hey," Marcie interrupted, "I think it's great, and it's certainly been easier on me since you stopped working sixteen hours a day."

"Speaking of work," Dani gave a soft chuckle, "what brought you out of your dungeon?"

"Chet Davis," Marcie told her. "He asked if you'd have time to see him this afternoon. Do you want me to set up a time for him?"

"No." Dani closed the unread folder on her desk.

"I'm not getting anything done here. I think I'll just go on down to his office."

A wraith of a young woman with vulnerable gray eyes looked up guiltily from a folder, stifling what suspiciously resembled a yawn as Dani entered Chet's outer office.

"Miss Simms," she said, "I ... We ..."

"You're Robyn, aren't you?" Dani asked gently.

She nodded.

"If Chet is such a slave driver that he's worn you down already, it's no wonder he can't keep a secretary," Dani teased in a light voice, sensing her embarrassment.

"Oh, no," Robyn stammered. "Mr. Davis is a wonderful boss." She flushed a bright red and dropped her glance to the folder on her desk. "It's just that I had a late date last night."

Having had a few late nights herself, Dani smiled sympathetically at the girl. "I know the feeling."

"D.J.!" Chet said as he stuck his head around the partially opened door. "What brings you to the catacombs? Come on in."

Raising an inquisitive eyebrow, Dani entered his office and crossed to the window, looking out over the city. "I'd hardly call the fifteenth floor the catacombs, Chet," she said dryly. "Although," she added, grimacing as she studied the stacks of folders on every available surface, "if you keep at it for a few more months, you probably will have a giant maze in this room."

He laughed good-naturedly and settled himself behind his desk. "Make yourself comfortable."

She scooted a stack of folders to one side and

perched on the credenza in front of the window. "Is Robyn going to be allowed to make any headway in this mess?" she drawled, "or are you going to chase her off before she has a chance to get it straightened out?"

"Robyn is the reason for this mess," he said, chuckling. "She convinced me my filing system was 'antiquated' and is now in the process of making my office as organized as the rest of the firm."

Dani gave a low whistle of appreciation. "If she can do that, you have found yourself a jewel."

"Yes. If I can just keep her."

"Problems already?"

"Not really," he said. "She wants to be a paralegal, and she's certainly bright enough, and ambitious enough, even though she is awfully young." He smiled grimly. "I'm going to have to recommend that we give her some tuition assistance just as soon—"

"As soon as she gets your files straightened out?" Dani said, laughing.

"That, too, and as soon as I'm convinced that this new boyfriend of hers isn't going to drag her off to Glenpool or Broken Arrow to start raising babies instead of pursuing a career."

"Poor Chet." Dani clucked in sympathy. "Either way, you'll be back in total disorganization within two weeks." Her eyes flashed with a delighted gleam. "But you can't have Marcie."

His laugh boomed through the room. "I knew you'd say that. That's why I didn't bother to ask." He picked the stub of a cigar from his ashtray and relit it. "But I do want to talk about Marcie. It's time for her annual evaluation."

"Already?" Dani asked. "It seems that it was just a few months ago that we went through this."

"No. That was the merit raise you recommended for her. Any problems?"

"You've got to be kidding. She keeps *me* organized. She gets my work out on time, she keeps her mouth shut about our clients, she pampers me, and even feeds my ego. No, I don't have any problems, Chet. In fact, she's so blasted competent that I sometimes wonder if she couldn't run things without me."

Dani twisted sideways on the credenza toward him, stricken by a disturbing thought. "Oh, Chet."

"What's the matter, D.J.?"

Dani massaged the back of her neck with one hand and studied the floor for a moment before speaking.

"With training, she wouldn't need me," she said finally. "I've felt so lucky to have her as a secretary, I never considered that she might want more of a career."

"Do you want me to recommend her for a promotion?"

"No." Dani shook her head slowly. "No. Not until I've talked to her. In the meantime, give her the raise she's earned, write up her annual report with lots of superlatives, and I'll be back in a couple of days to sign it."

Marcie, a slight frown on her face, was just hanging up the telephone when Dani stepped into her alcove.

"Trouble?" Dani asked.

"Not for us," Marcie said and sniffed. "Honestly, I don't know how those people at Win-Tech keep track of anything. That was Gene Speer from legal, calling me up to chew us out because they hadn't gotten their Creek County drilling opinion."

"What?" Dani demanded.

"That's what I said," Marcie told her. "I couriered that thing over to them, along with their abstracts, two weeks ago, but he wouldn't believe me until I pulled the receipt and read him the date and his secretary's name. Now he wants a copy of the opinion and the receipt." A smile broke across her face. "Oh, well," she said as she spread the prongs of the file folder and extracted the needed papers. "It could be worse. I could be his secretary."

"Marcie?" Dani was reluctant to say anything further, but it wouldn't be fair to the girl not to.

"Yes, D.J.?"

"Come into my office for a minute," she said slowly. "I need to talk to you."

Dani closed the hall door behind them and, instead of going to her desk, sat in the second visitor's chair, next to Marcie.

"You're very good at your job," she began hesitantly, "but I wonder if you're satisfied with what you're doing."

"Is there something I should know?" Marcie asked. She studied Dani intently, puzzlement clouding her normally open countenance.

"No," Dani reassured her. "It's just that it was brought home to me this afternoon that you have the ability to do more than transcribe my dictation. You've picked up enough knowledge that you could probably fill a paralegal slot right now, and if you wanted to continue your education, you wouldn't have any trouble with law school." Dani paused, troubled, trying to find words to ask Marcie if she wanted to be promoted.

Marcie's delighted laughter pealed through the room.

"I hope you're not trying to kick me up the corporate ladder," she said, still laughing, "because I won't let you."

Now it was Dani's turn to wear a puzzled frown.

"Look," Marcie told her, "I'm not a career woman; I'm just a housewife who needs a second income. And as long as I have to work, I'm happy working with you. I couldn't take the pressure you're under. Joe couldn't take it either. He's the most important thing in my world right now—not a promotion, not more money, and certainly not more responsibility that would cut into my time with him. Besides"—Marcie paused, nibbling on her lip—"I wasn't going to say anything for a while, but I don't know how much longer I'll be working."

Marcie walked to the window and looked down at the street.

"Joe isn't being transferred, is he?" Dani asked.

"No. He's traveling more than I like, but he's not being transferred." Marcie took a deep breath and turned to face Dani. A smile transformed her face. "I'm going to have a baby. That's why my doctor's appointment was so important last week."

Dani felt as though a lead weight had wedged itself in the back of her throat, pressing her down and backward, as she looked at the woman across the room. Marcie radiated joy as she stood outlined against the window. How could she tolerate watching such happiness, being constantly reminded...

She forced herself to smile, to appear pleased, to speak.

"That's wonderful."

"Yes." Marcie giggled once and then became serious. "D.J., I may not be able to quit work, but if I do, I'll help you choose my replacement, and I'll train her so well you won't even notice I'm gone."

Dani made a noise that should have been a laugh before she walked across the room and embraced the younger woman. "You've worked some miracles around here, Marcie," she said as she released her, "but I don't think even you are capable of doing that. I'll miss you."

She turned to her desk before Marcie could see how upset she was. "It's Friday," she said in a voice far brighter than she felt. "Why don't you give that Win-Tech mess to one of the couriers and then get out of here. Surprise Joe by beating him home for a change."

After Marcie left, Dani gripped the desk. "Won't even notice she's gone?" she whispered. Damn it! She knew better than to let herself care for someone, but the quiet friendship she felt for Marcie had developed so subtly that she hadn't even realized it was happening until it was full-blown and already a part of her life.

Dani remained subdued through dinner. Nick's best efforts merely evoked a halfhearted attempt at laughter from her. When she pleaded not feeling well, he took her home early, held her in the warmth of his arms for a moment, and then left her.

The next day, though, he refused to allow her any excuse.

"I don't know what's put you in this foul mood, but it's too perfect a day for anyone to be depressed. Put on your walking shoes," he demanded, "and grab a jacket and a scarf."

Dani suppressed a smile as she did what he told her. Someday she was going to have to have a talk with him about being so autocratic, but for now she didn't mind having someone telling her what to do.

The late morning bore all the promise of springtime. Across the courtyard, a maintenance man pushed a lawnmower, and the scent of fresh cut grass wafted through the air. Dani paused on the sidewalk, enjoying the warm breeze caressing her face, as she searched the parking area.

"What are you looking for?" Nick asked as he slipped his arm around her shoulder.

"Your car. Where did you have to park today?"

He grinned as he led her a few spaces and opened the passenger door of a sky blue Mercedes convertible.

"Your chariot, milady."

She sank into the leather seat and stretched her legs out in front of her, casting an appreciative glance around the interior of the car. When Nick slid into the driver's seat, she cocked an eyebrow at him but said nothing.

"This is strictly my fair-weather car," he said, answering her unspoken question. "I only bring it out when I can enjoy it the way it ought to be enjoyed." He turned the key and the engine purred to life. "You'd better tie on that scarf," he reminded her as he backed from the parking space.

She needed the light jacket he had told her to bring, for the mid-April air, though warm, still carried a hint of winter into the open car as Nick guided it through the system of multilane highways looping and crossing the city, accelerating until the breeze whipped at their faces, bringing a glow to Dani's cheeks and finally a laugh to her throat.

He turned off the highway and slowed to a more sedate pace as he followed the gently curving Riverside Drive along the same route Dani had taken to work the day she met him. This time, however, she allowed herself the luxury of truly enjoying the drive.

The first wave of spring flowers had passed its prime. Bright yellow forsythia, vivid pink Japanese quince, and equally showy redbud still reminded by scattered blossoms of their earlier glory, but dogwood abounded, as did iris in a pallette of colors from palest mauve to intense royal purple. Dani drank in the beauty of the morning, absorbing impressions of nature's awakening as well as impressions of joggers along the paths, and of the covert glances from the persons they passed. At some point she became aware of the picture she and Nick must be presenting as they sped along—that of a laughing, handsome couple without a care in the world. Why not? she wondered defiantly. If only for an hour, she would forget everything except enjoying what the day, and Nick, brought her.

She touched his cheek and when he turned to look at her she said simply, "Thank you."

He caught her hand and held it against his cheek as his answering smile played across his face. "My pleasure."

He whipped across the street and into a parking place near the overlook. Wordlessly, she joined him at the front of the car and hand in hand they wandered across the narrow park and down the levels of artificial embankment until they stood at the river's edge, wavelets lapping at their toes.

"Keystone is full," Nick said, mentioning the lake created by damning the river farther to the west.

"Mmm." Dani leaned against a piling and watched a solitary gull dipping down over the water.

"Do you sail?"

"No," Dani murmured, engrossed in the beauty of the day and the play of light across the broad expanse of river.

Nick retrieved a pebble from near his feet and skimmed it across the water. "I'll have to teach you. I think you'd enjoy it."

"I think I probably would," Dani admitted. "I've always felt the call of water. It seems, somehow, emotionally cleansing."

Nick skimmed another pebble across the water before turning toward her, a question in his eyes. "Dani—"

"Mommy!" The child's high-pitched wail paralyzed Dani for a moment, until she forced herself to turn toward the sound. On the level above them stood a little girl, silver hair clouding her face, a vision in pink corduroy, and utterly terrified. "Mommy!" she screamed again before running toward the steps. The child's foot slipped, and she slithered on hands and knees across the rough surface of the terrace.

Dani whirled and scrambled up the steps to her, kneeling beside her almost as the child stopped sliding.

"Ssh, baby, it's all right," she crooned as she gathered the little girl to her. "It's all right. We'll find your mommy."

She jerked the scarf from her neck and began drying the child's tears, murmuring soft words to the girl until her sobs eased and the child looked up at her, a tremulous smile on her streaked face. Only then was Dani aware of Nick beside her, holding out his handkerchief, which, while she had been busy with the child, he had managed to dampen.

"Let's see those hands now." Dani teased the little

girl until she opened her fists for her. "Can you tell me your name?" she asked as she washed dirt from the scratches.

"Jen-fer," the child sobbed.

"Jennifer. That's a pretty name." She worked steadily, checking for serious injury, but there seemed to be only mild scratches. "How old are you?"

Jennifer held up three stubby fingers. "This many."

"Three," Dani said. She washed back a wave of weakness that threatened to overcome her, feeling suddenly that all warmth had gone from the day.

She almost whispered the words, "Your mommy must be proud of you." She caressed the child's cheek. "You're an awfully nice little girl."

"You're nice, too," Jennifer said matter-of-factly. "What happened to *your* hands?"

Although Nick stood beside her, his voice seemed to come from a great distance. "I'll bet that's your mommy over there, little girl. Can you walk? Give me your hand and I'll help you up the steps."

Gratefully, she heard the noises of their footsteps fading, the murmurs of the reunion, and Jennifer's giggle receding as she was carried away.

Nick's hands on her shoulders reminded her that she still knelt on the embankment, staring blindly at her hands. She let him help her to her feet before she stuffed her tightly balled fists into her jacket pockets.

"There's no reason to do that," he said softly.

She looked at him blankly and swallowed, trying to ease the tightness in her throat.

He held out his hands for hers and reluctantly she pulled them from her pockets and let him clasp them.

"Unless someone cares enough about you to look

closely, the scars aren't noticeable. And once he cares
that much, he ceases to see them.'' He drew her hands
toward him and placed a gentle kiss on the back of each
one. Then he brushed the hair away from her face and
traced the line of almost invisible scars along her hairline with his fingers before bending to her and following the path of his fingers with fleetingly soft kisses.

"I didn't think you'd seen those,'' she whispered.

"Dani, I notice everything about you.''

"But you never gave any indication—''

He spoke in a voice that was more caress than words, a
voice which took all sting from what he said. ''What was
I going to say? Tell me about the pain? No. I had hoped
that someday you'd feel free enough with me to want to
talk about it, but until that time I wasn't going to pry.''

Now was the time to tell him. Dani knew that as she
leaned against him. Now, before she cared too much.
Now, before losing him would really matter. Now. And
yet, she could not speak the words which would take
the comfort of his arms from her, which would leave
her alone and empty as she had been just a few short
days ago.

A tremor shook her, and Nick drew her closer. ''So
much for my carefully laid plans to cheer you up,'' he
said in a voice lightly laced with irony. ''What else can I
do to make the day worse?''

She shook her head against his chest before she
placed her fingers on his lips to quiet him. He had done
nothing wrong

His lips moved over her fingers, teasing them, sending shivers of delight down her arm to merge with the
ache growing within her.

She looked up at him to find him watching her, his

eyes darkened and softened by an emotion she refused to explore. Too late. It was already too late not to matter. Bereft by the loss she felt, knowing that soon he would leave, taking with him that special joy of living she had too briefly shared, she felt the chill creeping over her. Insidiously, as though playing with its power, the trembling followed. She fought it, willing herself not to let it happen, but it was too late for that, too. The emotions in Nick's eyes were easy to read now—shock, followed by concern. She could no longer bear to watch the changes in his face.

"Dani, what is it? What's wrong?"

She closed her eyes and stood huddled against her misery, wondering if she would ever be able to answer him. "Take me home, Nick. Please."

Although she protested it wasn't necessary, he insisted on putting the top on the car, as he insisted on turning on the heater. Nothing seemed to help. He drove quickly, his knuckles white against the steering wheel. She stumbled as he helped her from the car, and he grasped her securely about the waist and hurried her into the apartment where he gently, but forcefully, seated her on the couch.

"Don't move."

She heard noises as he moved about the bedroom, felt the warmth of the blanket being tucked around her, heard him moving in the kitchen, and then felt the cold rim of a glass being held to her lips.

"Drink this."

She swallowed automatically, choking when the unexpected harshness of the liquid hit her throat.

"Mama Giuseppina's wine," he said gently. "It's the only thing I could find. Drink it all."

Obediently, she drank until he took the glass from her and set it on the coffee table. He drew her down on the sofa, tucking the blanket securely around her, kneeling beside her as he smoothed her hair away from her face and began massaging her arms through the layers of wool and clothing, soothing her much as she had earlier soothed Jennifer.

Why didn't he just go away and leave her to get through this by herself? It would pass. Everything passed—if you gave it enough time, if you worked hard enough at pushing it out of your life.

No! That wasn't what she wanted! Then what did she want? Right now it was his warmth next to her, the caress of his hands, and the soft murmur of his voice. Right now it was taking the comfort he gave her, as she had taken it that first night, as she had taken it in some form daily since they met. Taking, always taking...

She forced herself to look at him, to meet the unspoken questions in his eyes. He had asked nothing from her, and in exchange for all he had given her, was even now giving, that was exactly what she had given in return. Nothing.

She struggled to free her arms from the soft prison of the blanket, ignoring his gentle protests as she pulled herself to a sitting position. She twined her arms around him and gradually, cradled by him, she felt warmth returning. She breathed deeply and leaned back against the sofa, weak but no longer trembling, still supported by his protective embrace.

"Dani," he said shakily, "you scared the hell out of me."

"Sometimes," she told him, finding it difficult to speak, "I frighten myself."

But the fright he spoke of was tempered by concern for her. She could sense it in the way he still held her, in the puzzled set of his mouth, in the depths of his eyes. Concern for her, care for her, and...

His eyes held her mesmerized. Their green lights drank from her and nourished her. They held the world at bay while drawing her ever closer to him. They spoke without words to a chord within her more elemental than thought.

She touched his cheek and outlined his brows with tentative fingers before cupping his face in her hands.

"Nick?"

They moved toward each other in unison, as though each had been waiting, as though something within told them that this was their moment. Their mouths met in mutual need, voicing their own, answering the other's, until that contact was not enough and they moved closer, unable yet to get close enough to satisfy the hunger within them. They explored each other, each pleasure intensified by their sharing. As they freed themselves of clothing, the branding of flesh against flesh amplified each celebration of mouth and hand.

Dani was beyond thought, lost in a world where nothing existed but Nick and now, driven only by the hunger that threatened to consume her and by a visceral need to satisfy Nick's matching hunger.

When he pulled away from her, she moaned in frustration. She tried to draw him to her, but he remained poised above her, his eyes heavy with passion, his breathing ragged.

"Dani, are you sure?"

She murmured an inarticulate sound as she tried to raise herself to capture his lips. He held her down.

"Then say it," he whispered. "I have to hear you say it."

She was incapable of clear thought, but she tried to understand what he was asking. Was this some kind of punishment? Did he have to have some sort of ego reinforcement because of what had happened the first time? It didn't matter. None of that mattered now. She forced the words through the tightness of her throat.

"Make love to me, Nick. Please." When he made no move, she looked up at him wildly. "I want you," she moaned. "Oh, God, I want you."

He did not sound victorious when he spoke. If anything, his voice was edged with sadness. A rueful smile twisted his mouth. "That's a start," he said as he bent to her.

He touched her lips lightly, tracing them with his fingers—a moment of tentative gentleness, as though giving her one last chance to reconsider. But it was not gentleness she needed now. It was the hard pressure of his body against hers. She arched upward, craving that contact, needing release from the awesome hunger within her.

He moaned her name as he captured her mouth with his, giving her the possessiveness she demanded. He moved against her, his hands, his lips, his body all instruments of exquisite torture as he drew her farther and farther into their own private world—a world comprised only of the feelings of his muscles beneath her hands, his flesh against hers, his taste in her mouth, and the wondrous agonies of pleasure that he continued to build and build and build, until she hung suspended in an eternal moment so intense that all feeling, all thought, all movement stopped, brought to life only by the cry that tore from her throat. She felt the tremors coursing through his body as she felt her own, and still they held each other, locked in an embrace neither moved to end.

Sometime later, sated and wondering, they moved to her bed, holding each other in hushed contentment. Sometime later they turned to each other again. Again there was no past to shadow, no future to cloud. There was only the two of them, now, giving to each other, and the heights they scaled were no less awesome, no less shattering than the ones they had traveled such a short time before.

Dani curled into him, nestling her cheek against his chest, throwing one arm across him and clasping his waist. With the fingers of one hand he traced lazy circles on her thigh while with the other arm he secured her against him.

She drifted langorously for only moments before her eyes grew heavy and she slid into dreamless sleep. When she awoke—hours later? minutes later?—feeling boneless and liquid, they still held each other. Somewhere in the distance, just beyond the range of recognition, she heard music playing. Were there violins? she wondered. How silly, she realized as her lips curved in a secret smile. If she wanted violins, of course there would be violins.

How truly wonderful it felt to be free of that persistent cold knot that had seemed to lodge itself permanently in her midsection.

She moved her hand tentatively, loving the feel of Nick's supple skin beneath her fingers, tracing a path across his flat stomach, through the crisp mat that veed down his chest, to his shoulder, and finally burrowing her fingers in the soft dark hair at the back of his head and pulling herself even closer to him.

He tightened his hand on her hip. His other hand smoothed the hair away from her face so he could trail teasing kisses over the moist skin of her forehead and cheek.

Was it possible? she wondered. Could he be feeling the same delightful glow? She twisted so that she could see his face, and she read in his expression what she knew was a reflection of her own, the subtly shadowed eyes, the absence of any lines of tension, the softly curving lips.

"I was starving, Nick," she said, her voice low and urgent, "and I didn't even know it."

"There's no reason for that, Dani." He lifted her and settled her along the length of him, his hands molding her to the contours of his body. He pushed aside her heavy mane of hair that veiled both their faces with its silken strands. "Not ever again."

Soft gray light filtered through the drawn curtains of the bedroom as Dani felt Nick easing his arm from under her. Half asleep, she murmured in protest and reached for him.

He feathered a kiss across her closed eyelids. "I'll be right back."

He tucked the sheet over her. She heard noises from the living room, and then he returned, sliding into bed beside her but pushing the pillow against the headboard and leaning against it. She snuggled toward him, eyes closed, and heard the snap of his cigarette lighter, smelled the once again tempting aroma of tobacco

smoke, and felt the movement of his chest as he exhaled deeply.

He held her close to his side. The change in him was
so subtle it was a few moments before she noticed it.
It was as though he had withdrawn from her. There was
a wariness, a tension about the way he sat and about the
way he held her. She opened her eyes to look up at him
and found him watching her, but she wasn't sure he
actually saw her.

"What's wrong?" she asked.

He smiled an endearing half smile, stubbed out his
cigarette, and pulled her up beside him, keeping her
securely within the confines of his arm. "Not a thing."

But there was something wrong. She could sense it.
And he only added to her growing uneasiness when he
lit another cigarette. He still held her, but his attention
seemed to be focused somewhere beyond the clouds of
smoke.

Suddenly, embarrassingly aware of her nakedness
and of the abandonment with which she had responded to him, she plucked at the sheet, pulling it up
over her.

"Cold?" he asked.

"Yes," she lied.

He looked down at her and for a moment she
thought he was going to take her in his arms with an
offer to help keep her warm. Instead, he said, "Let me
get your robe for you. Where is it?"

"In the closet."

He rose from the bed but before crossing to the
closet door he walked into the living room. When he
returned, he had already put on his slacks and slipped

into his shirt, although the shirt remained unbuttoned and hung open.

He walked into the closet, flipped on the light, and was silent.

"Can't you find it?" Dani asked, her voice unnaturally tight. "It's right by the door."

Nick's reply was mumbled from inside the closet. "I'm looking for Old Faithful."

"What?"

"Old Faithful—the beat up, warm one you put on when you're by yourself. All I can find is this blue satin thing."

He continued talking, although she only half heard what he said.

"How do you keep your closet so organized? Where's the clutter that's supposed to be around women's clothes?"

With Old Faithful, she thought as a lump caught in her throat, and she sank back against the pillow while unwanted memories threatened to intrude. She took a quick, deep breath and forced the images away.

"The blue one will have to do," she said too brightly. "I'm afraid it's the only one I have."

He brought the robe to her and helped her slip into it. He caught her upper arms in his hands when he did so and looked at her with what was almost a smile. He brushed a kiss across her forehead and released her. "I think it's time to raid the kitchen."

Intuition urged her to remain silent, to wait for him to give her some indication of what was bothering him.

She followed him into the tiny kitchen and reached for the coffeepot.

"Oh, no," he said, lifting her up and depositing her

on a bar stool in front of the narrow breakfast bar. "I do the work. You can criticize if you want to."

Deftly, he measured grounds and water into the pot and started the brew cycle. Then he scavenged through the refrigerator and pantry, frowning slightly before making a decision and piling various items on the counter.

"Griddle?" he asked.

"No," Dani told him. "Just a skillet. Lower left."

He bent down and captured the skillet. "Organized kitchen, too," he said. "Aren't you supposed to have a jumble of unused pots and pans?"

"That's a myth," Dani said as she attempted to smile, "probably fostered by men who can't find their way around in a kitchen, no matter how organized it is."

He grinned at her, and she realized that he was neatly tucking away whatever it was that had been bothering him and returning to the easy, companionable manner she had grown to rely upon.

He cracked eggs into the skillet. "I thought I'd dazzle you with my eggs Benedict, but you're not set up for it, so we'll have to settle for the cheap imitation."

He worked quickly, juggling the eggs, the Canadian bacon, and the English muffins in the skillet, building the sandwiches as though it was something he did frequently. He added sliced cheese before topping each with a muffin half and sliding them onto plates just as the coffee maker gave its groan of completion. He poured two cups, handed one to her, and settled himself on the adjacent bar stool.

"Eat," he urged when she sat silently watching him. "They're guaranteed to be better than the advertised ones."

And they were. "You're a man of many talents, Mr. Sanders," she said as she picked up a last piece of muffin from her plate and popped it into her mouth.

He leaned over and planted a light kiss on her lips. "I'm glad you realize that," he said as he picked up their plates and carried them to the sink.

"Nick?"

He paused, holding one plate under running water, and turned to her. No. She couldn't ask him, no matter how she wondered about his changing attitude. If she began asking him questions, she'd have to give him the right to ask of her things she couldn't answer.

"Nothing," she said. "It's just..." She hesitated, searching for words. "It's just that I know it hasn't been easy for you to be around me, not understanding why I sometimes act the way I do. I..."

He turned the water off and gave her his full attention, looking intently into her eyes as she spoke.

"I..." She knew she ought to stop, but she couldn't. "Why did you put up with me as long as you did?"

She thought he must be having as much trouble finding words as she had been. His look played over her face, questioning her, before softening.

He walked to her and cupped her chin in his hand. "Because I'm in love with you," he said softly.

She felt the blood draining from her face, felt the leaden heaviness of her heart and the quick catch of breath that muffled her whimpered, "No."

She tried to turn away from him, but he held her face prisoner in his hands.

"I think I fell in love with you the moment you grabbed my hand to keep me from lunging across the table after Sam Wilson."

"It's too soon." Her voice was no more than a whisper. "You can't be sure."

"Dani, I'm thirty-seven. Old enough to know how I feel. And I know I've never felt this way about another person in my life. I love you. Is that so awful?"

She twisted away from him, breaking the paralyzing influence of his gaze, tearing herself from the tantalizing touch of his fingers on her skin. "I never meant for this to happen."

And she hadn't. As she frantically searched her conscience, she knew that not once had she even considered that he might fall in love with her. He couldn't be serious. She held onto that thought. He was only exaggerating, perhaps not even consciously, the closeness they had seemed to develop. But it had to end, and now, before he became too firmly convinced that what he felt was love, before both of them were hurt. She wasn't sure she could survive again.

"Don't tell me you don't feel anything," he said from behind her. "I won't believe you. Not after today."

She stared at an imaginary spot on the wall and swallowed hard. "The sex was very good—"

"What?" He twisted her violently around to face him. "The sex was very good! Is that all it meant to you? Just an exercise in the bedroom?"

"No!" she cried. "I like you, Nick..." She closed her eyes against the golden daggers shooting from his. "I care for you. But I don't—I *can't*—love you."

"I see," he said grimly. "There's no clutter in your closet or your kitchen. There's no clutter in your life either, is there? No room for any extraneous matter, such as human emotions? I'm sorry, Dani. I thought

I'd seen something different in you. I guess I was wrong."

She sat numbly while he finished dressing, yanking on his shoes and angrily stuffing his shirttail into his slacks.

It was better this way, she told herself. Better that it end now. Better that they never see each other again. *Better than what?* her heart screamed as he strode toward the door.

She was not aware of crossing the room. Without knowing how she got there, she found herself between Nick and the door. He stopped, waiting for her to speak.

"Nick." Her words were free creatures, acting against any order her rational mind could give. "Please, don't leave me."

He sighed in defeat. "You've got my guts so tied in knots now that half the time I don't know what I'm doing. Just what do you want from me?"

She looked at him in silence for long seconds, and then, acknowledging defeat herself, she tipped her head forward to rest on his chest. "I don't know."

The silence crushed in on her as she stood passively before him. She felt the tremor that worked through him before he gathered her in his arms. "Then," he murmured against her hair, "I guess we'd better find out."

Chapter Six

With Nick, Dani discovered, finding out proved to be a delightful experience, as long as she didn't let herself think about what she was doing and just did it. He captured her time, filling her waking hours, and her sleeping hours, with excitement.

The hours she spent at the office, instead of being her reason for living now became hours that she must endure until she could again be with Nick. She began, for the first time, to understand Marcie's attitude. Pangs of guilt occasionally nipped at her for not getting as much done as she once had, but she learned to cope with those, grinning ruefully as she realized she was still turning out more work than anyone else would have expected had she not set such a driven pace for herself long before.

She wondered, at times, how Nick managed his schedule to have so much time for her. But she wasn't going to complain, and she certainly wasn't going to remind him that he ought to have more important things to do than spend hours with her, hours that started out lazy and relaxed and evolved into ecstasy.

As if by mutual consent they avoided discussions of

their childhoods. Dani found little that was amusing to relate about her succession of foster homes. Nick seemed reluctant to tell her more than he had been raised in a home that was essentially fatherless—even before his father had died in an accident, because his father had followed the oil fields, and that his mother now lived in Los Angeles with his brother's family.

The past didn't matter. There were too many new discoveries being made. The sinful luxury of having him fill the tub with water just the right temperature for her, hand her a chilled glass of wine, and then, grinning wickedly, slide into the tub with her, completely destroying any illusion of relaxation. The secret knowledge they shared as they sat with hands locked together in the concert hall, knowing they would feel the music long after the musicians had gone home. The delight that she took in learning, and he took in teaching her, the new dance steps. The awareness that his lightest touch or the fanning of his breath against her skin could draw her into a vortex of mindless pleasure and—wonder of wonders—that she seemed to have the same ability to ignite his response. No. There were too many wonderful new discoveries to allow the past to intrude.

Lynde's, at the top of the tallest Brady Center Tower, appeared much the same as it had the first night they were there. The change was in her, Dani realized. With the russet silk swirling about her ankles, her hair cascading over her shoulders, and Nick's arm securely about her waist, she was a far different person from the businesslike shell who had walked through this same door only weeks before.

The table overlooking the lights of the city awaited them. Nick paused only to order before taking her hand in his and leading her to the dance floor. Knowing the rhythm of each other's body as they now did, they moved with a fluidity that surpassed that earlier time. And now she felt free to revel in the sensations generated as his body moved with hers and against hers, as she felt free, later, to take his hand as it lay beside hers on the table, free to smile a sensual promise at him as they whispered and laughed together over dinner. When he drew her to her feet after dinner to lead her again to the dance floor, she felt free to slide her arm around his waist and lean confidently close to him as they walked the short distance.

At the top of the steps to the polished floor, Nick paused, and even through the soft fabric of his jacket, Dani felt his muscles tighten under her hand. Puzzled by the abrupt tension in him, she looked up to see an incredibly hard expression in his eyes as he stared across the room. She glanced in the direction of his gaze, toward a candle-lit table on the edge of the dance floor. It took a moment for her to assimilate what she saw, and then the implications hit her and she tightened her hand on Nick's waist.

Sam Wilson sat at the table, his handsome profile toward them so that he did not seem aware of their presence. He spoke quietly but insistently with the woman seated opposite him, a woman whose face had been indelibly engraved on Dani's memory that night at the restaurant when she first saw her, a stunning redhead with patrician features who now studied Nick as a cheshire cat smile twisted her lips.

Time stood still for them until Nick applied gentle

pressure to her spine and urged her down the steps. He gathered her into the easy embrace of dance. "Now do you understand why he did it?" he asked.

"No," Dani told him. "If anything, I understand less than I did before I saw him with your ex-wife."

"It wasn't the paycheck he wanted, Dani. It was the satisfaction of putting something over on me. And it doesn't make much difference at this point whether it was his idea or hers."

He led her through a complicated series of steps before she felt the anger and tension leave him. As he drew her to him, she felt his whisper brushing her cheek. "Poor bastard."

"Why do you say that?"

"He's not strong enough for her. She'll have him doing things he never dreamed of doing, tolerating situations that are intolerable. She'll break him."

Had she tried that with Nick? Had that been what finally destroyed their marriage? Dani missed a step and stumbled lightly toward him.

"Don't worry about them, Dani," Nick told her softly. "Neither one of them is worthy of your worry."

She wouldn't. She determined that as she leaned against him and let the music carry them away from all thoughts of Marilyn or Sam Wilson. But they intruded after the next dance, a fast jazz tune that left her breathless and flushed. Laughing together, she and Nick were returning to their table when Dani caught sight of Marilyn watching her.

Fully aware of how disheveled she must be after the exertion of the last dance, Dani drew a mental comparison between herself and the immaculately coiffed and made-up perfection of Nick's ex-wife and made a quick decision. When they reached their table, Nick pulled out her chair for her, but she shook her head and reached for her purse.

"I'm going to freshen up," she told him lightly. "I'll be right back."

She moved with apparent confidence across the room, inwardly berating herself for the insecurity she felt. After all, Marilyn was his *ex*-wife. And Nick had made it obvious that he had a very low opinion of the woman. Why, then, was Dani so concerned about not suffering in comparison with her?

But she was, she admitted as she sank onto the padded bench in front of the lighted mirrors of the ladies' lounge and dragged her comb through her heavy hair. She heard the soft sounds of the door opening and the rustle of fabric, looked absently in the mirror, and then froze, her comb suspended in midstroke. Marilyn stood behind her. Clad in a glittering green sheath that matched her eyes, she leaned casually and yet somehow ominously against the closed door.

"Wise move, Miss Simms," she said, nodding toward the still suspended comb. "Nick always liked his women to be tidy."

Dani dragged the comb through her hair one more time before tossing it in her purse and snatching the tube of lip gloss. Patience, she told herself. The woman obviously wanted something. She steadied her hand and applied the gloss.

"Of course, you are a wise young woman, aren't you? You've promoted yourself from his"—Marilyn paused between the words—"lawyer to his dancing partner. I assume you fill his other needs as well."

Dani slid the cap on the gloss and swiveled to face

Marilyn. A cold rage was building in her at the effrontery of this woman, but she steeled herself in her best courtroom manner and spoke icily. "You may *assume* anything you wish. I have no control over that."

"But do you have any control over Nick?" Marilyn's gaze raked over Dani. "I see no jewelry. Does that mean you haven't yet managed to inveigle any presents from him—no tokens of his affection?"

Dani felt her rage building. How dare this woman intrude on her privacy and insult her? And insult Nick. It seemed as though she found nothing to value in Nick himself, only in what his money could buy. Dani snapped her purse shut and rose to leave. Marilyn was taller than she had thought, and she stood solidly blocking the door.

"I see no reason to continue this discussion," Dani said. "Please step aside."

"Oh, but I'm not through," Marilyn insisted in a maddeningly calm voice. "I want to make sure, before I leave you to his tender mercies, that you understand just how profitable a relationship with Nick can be."

Dani marveled at the feeling growing within her, a good healthy anger such as she had not known in years. "I'm not exactly destitute," she said.

"No, dear. I didn't mean to say that you were. But being 'not exactly destitute' and having access to Nick's considerable fortune are two completely different things. And you need to know, before you become too dependent upon Nick's bounty, that it can be dangerous to you."

"Are you threatening me?" Dani asked with a calm she did not feel.

Marilyn's laughter pealed through the room. "Me?

No, I'm warning you. Apparently, you haven't seen it yet, but Nick does have his darker side. My dear Miss Simms, your only danger will come from him."

What could she call this woman? She wanted to hurl a name at her, and she'd be damned if it would be Mrs. Sanders.

"You speak from experience, of course." The words dripped with saccharine.

"You little fool!" Marilyn snapped. "I'm warning you that Nick can be violent. Play him for all you want, but don't be surprised if he turns on you when you don't do what he wants, when he wants."

Violent? Dani had no doubt that Marilyn had been able to provoke him to violence. After five minutes with her, anyone would be provoked to violence.

"Get out of my way," Dani said as she moved toward the door.

"And if I choose not to—yet?"

Dani looked at the woman, thankful for the first time for her street wise and tomboyish childhood that Mrs. Simms, her former mother-in-law, had never failed to throw up to her. "You're at least six inches taller than I am, and you outweigh me by more than twenty pounds, but if you don't move away from that door, now, you're going to find out that you're not the only woman in this room who knows how to fight dirty."

Marilyn smiled lazily, but she moved to the side of the door. "And Dani," she said as Dani opened the door, "ask him about the divorce. Or better yet, read the file. Frank Merriweather handled it for him."

Dani jerked the door closed behind her and strode down the hall. The nerve of that woman! Nick had been married to *her*? *Why?* Ask him about the divorce? She couldn't do that. She wouldn't want to ask him to drag forth the wounds of his marriage any more than she would want him to—

She clutched at the wall in sudden weakness. Any more than she would want him to probe at the wounds of hers. *God!* She hadn't thought of it once that entire day. She leaned her head against the wall and took a deep breath. And she wouldn't think of it now. She straightened her shoulders and stepped into the dining room.

From the doorway she could see Nick watching for her at their table across the room. Undoubtedly, he had seen Marilyn follow her. She fixed a smile on her face and worked at calming herself as she made her way to his side.

"Are you all right?" he asked as he pulled the chair out for her.

Dani saw no need to hide what had happened. "I've had a decidedly unpleasant experience," she said.

Nick rested his hands on her shoulders for a moment before he sat down and took her hand in his. The questions in his troubled eyes urged her to continue, but Dani hesitated. Marilyn's comments weren't worth repeating. Still, he seemed to want to know...need to know.

Dani smiled grimly. "She warned me to be wary of your violence in my campaign to gain access to your checkbook."

"And that was all?" he asked tensely.

"Essentially. But I think I left before she had said all she wanted." Dani realized for the first time just how she had managed to leave, and a chuckle of surprise broke from her. "As a matter-of-fact," she told Nick sheepishly, "I think I threatened her with a little violence of my own if she didn't let me leave."

Nick squeezed her hand resting in his and shook his head. A smile worked at his mouth, but his eyes remained troubled. "And are you now going to demand explanations from me?" he asked.

The decision had already been made. Dani no longer had to consider it. With her free hand she traced a line from the outer corner of his eye, down his jaw, and across to his lower lip. "No."

"Do you want to leave?"

Dani did not have to consider that question. It could be uncomfortable to remain under observation and yet to leave now would only give Marilyn an unearned sense of satisfaction.

"Not because of them," Dani said finally. "I think we've seen the worst either of them has to offer, and I refuse to let them spoil my time with you."

Her hand rested on his cheek. He turned his face into it and placed a kiss in her palm. "Good girl."

Dani had sounded much more confident than she felt. When Nick again led her to the dance floor, she was aware of Marilyn's watchful gaze. As they paused on the edge of the floor before moving into the dance, Sam Wilson turned toward her, a thin smile tightening his face as he nodded a grim salute. But all thoughts of the other couple faded as she moved with Nick to the haunting strains of "Night and Day."

"I'll never be able to hear this song again without thinking of you," Nick told her as he pulled her close.

Later, when they reluctantly returned to their table, Dani saw that Marilyn and Wilson were gone.

Nick arrived at her apartment Saturday morning dressed in faded jeans, cowboy boots, and a nondescript shirt with the sleeves rolled up to expose the bronzed strength of his arms. He raised a quizzical eyebrow and looked skeptically at the beige linen slacks and coral silk shirt she wore.

"You haven't gotten a pair of jeans yet?" he asked.

She'd sworn that she'd never again wear jeans, but the reasons for that oath became more obscure each time he teased her.

She shook her head, and he grimaced in mock dismay. "Well, don't say you weren't warned. Are you ready to leave?"

Dani raised her cup to her lips for one last sip of coffee as she asked, "Where are we going?"

"We're going to drill an oil well."

She choked on the coffee and while he obligingly pounded on her back, she caught her breath. "Nick, this weekend is only two days long. I don't think even you can drill a well before Monday."

He eased the pressure on her back to a gentle massage and laughed softly. "No," he admitted. "At least not where I want to drill. All we'll do today is stake and build the location."

She shook her head. "Aren't you forgetting a few things?"

"What?"

She listed the items on her fingers. "Oh, just leases, title opinions, pooling orders, spacing orders, and drilling permits."

"No. I haven't forgotten them," he said and, maddeningly, said no more.

"You're surely not just going to ignore them, are you?"

"Come on, counselor. You don't have to be a lawyer today. Finish your coffee and I'll explain everything on the way out to the drill site."

The reason he didn't have to worry about her list of necessities, he told her as they sped west into Creek County, was that this particular location was part of a large lease he had taken years before and on which he already had three producing oil wells. Everything had been taken care of long ago, except for obtaining the permit to drill, and he considered that a formality that would give him no trouble.

They turned south off the highway and followed a graveled road for several miles before Nick turned in at an open gate. Inside the gate, two men were off-loading a bulldozer from a flatbed trailer, and Nick stopped the car and walked over to speak with the men. When he returned to the car, he carried a hammer and a wooden stake.

"Now comes the hard part," he said as he eased his long frame back into the car. "I have to decide where we're going to drill this hole."

"You don't know?" Dani said and laughed. "What about the experts that you told me you surrounded yourself with? Didn't your geologists have any suggestions?"

"Sure," he said, laughing, too. "The reason I went after this lease in the first place was that my geologists were certain that there is a—quote, unbelievable, end of quote—channel of Red Fork Sand, which contains a prehistoric riverbed chock-full of dead dinosaurs, running under this property. The problem is that although they all say it has to be here, none of them seem to agree on where *here* is."

They passed a black pump jack, moving up and down slowly in cadence with the rhythmic beat of an engine, resembling, Dani thought with a giggle, one of those silly gooney-bird drinking toys of her childhood. The site around the pump was scrupulously clean, devoid of any of the clutter and trash she had heard often existed around wells. To one side there sat a series of storage tanks, each gleaming white and bearing Nick's blue-and-white logo, an elongated diamond with the starkly modern initials of N.S.

"Don't let the size of that tank battery impress you," Nick said as they drove past. "It holds the production from all the wells on this lease. That well," he nodded toward the one they had just passed, "was the first. No Red Fork, or at least none to speak of. It's pumping out a whopping twenty-five barrels a day. Over there"—he pointed toward another pump jack barely visible to the south of them—"is the second. Missed it again. Ten barrels. Up in the northeast corner of the lease."

Dani looked in that direction but could see nothing.

Nick grinned at her unspoken question. "I have had my share of dry holes, Dani. That's just one of them."

The road was now little more than a trail through the sparse grass. "We did a little better on Number Four. It had a showing of Red Fork, but nothing like we expected, and we're not producing from that sand."

"But everyone is still sure it's here?" she teased.

"Yep. And since our friend Sam Wilson has temporarily set back my plans to go big game hunting in Beckham County, I figured I might as well look for it one more time."

He stopped the car at a badly eroded ditch. "This is as far as we can drive until after we get the road built." He walked around the car and opened the door for her, helping her out. "Watch where you step," he said, frowning as he looked at her high-heeled sling pumps.

"Yes, sir." She gave him a smart salute and then reached back into the car for the stake and hammer. "Don't forget these."

He took the hammer from her. "You keep the stake. I'm going to let you decide where to put it anyway."

"Me!" The word came out in a yelp. "Nick Sanders, I know you're crazy now. If your geologists can't tell you where to drill, what makes you think I can?"

He grasped her elbow and led her down into the gulley and back up the other side. The grass on this side was as sparse as that which they had driven through. While the whole countryside was growing green and lush, this pasture had only tufts of green showing. Dani had heard about overgrazing but had never seen the damage it could do. She looked around her in dismay. It was as though the grass had been ripped out of the ground, leaving only hardy weeds and flattened mounds of dried, adobelike cow droppings as evidence that it had ever been able to grow anything.

"I know," Nick said, as though reading her mind. "But I don't own the surface of the land, Dani. I can't control what happens to any of it, except for a small area around the wells.

"Come on," he said. "We don't have far to go." He kept a secure grasp on her arm as they made their way down the dusty red ruts of a tractor trail. "You really don't have much of a decision to make," he told her, reminding her of his earlier threat that she would determine the well location. "After reading the logs and studying the production of the neighboring wells, we've narrowed it down to three possibilities."

"And am I supposed to say, 'eenie, meenie, minie, moe,' or toss a coin?" she asked.

"Whatever method you want," he said, apparently unaware of the flip manner she questioned him. "You bring me luck, Dani, and that's what I need more than anything else. This is an educated man's game of blind man's bluff at this point."

Dani pulled loose from his grasp and stood in the roadway. "Nick, you can't be serious."

He only nodded at her, and the expression on his face told her he was.

"Listen to me," she said. "There's no way I can make that decision. For all I know about production or geology or engineering, I might as well close my eyes, spin around, and throw this stake."

He grinned at her, a sparkle lighting his eyes, but he didn't say anything.

She wouldn't make a decision of this magnitude for him. She couldn't! But maybe the only way to convince him of that was to prove her irresponsibility. She frowned at him and stepped out of the rut into a bare plot of red dirt.

"All right!" she snapped at him. She'd do it and then he could pick up the stake and put it where he wanted it. She squeezed her eyes shut. "Get out of my way," she told him. She'd play this silly game to the hilt. It was kind of fun, she admitted as she twirled around. Rather like pin-the-tail on the donkey. She twirled until she lost all sense of direction, stopped long enough to regain her balance, drew back her arm, and hurled the stake with all her strength. "There!" she cried as she opened her eyes.

Nick's shoulders were shaking with barely suppressed laughter, and the green lights in his eyes danced wickedly as he advanced on her.

"Now do you see how silly it was to expect me to choose your location?"

He nodded, not speaking, and guided her to the stake. It lay against a clump of weeds, but its pointed end rested squarely in the center of a large dry cow dropping.

Nick reached for the stake, but instead of picking it up he merely straightened it and began hammering it into the ground, through the center of the cow chip.

"What are you doing?"

He could no longer control his laughter. It broke from him, muffling his words. "I'm staking your well."

"Nick! What about your three possibilities? You can't just poke a hole in the ground because that's where the silly stake landed."

He kept on hammering, and laughing, and Dani began to realize he was serious.

"Nick!" She couldn't just stand by and let him spend his time and his money drilling a well there.

"Actually," he said, straightening himself to his full height and trying to bring his laughter under control, "it's not so far from one of the three possibilities that we'll even have to get a spacing variance. A name change is in order though."

He dropped the hammer and hugged her to him, going off again in fresh gales of laughter. "I wonder how the *very* staid and *very* proper Corporation Commission is going to react to an intent to drill the 'Cow Chip Number One?'"

"You wouldn't?"

"Watch," he told her, spinning her around.

It was hopeless. He was hopeless. He was going to drill the well where it was staked, and he was going to tag it with that ridiculous name, and there was nothing she could do about it. Except enjoy it. *Enjoy it!*

She felt her laughter building and let it bubble forth to mingle with his until it overpowered her, leaving her leaning helplessly against him and holding her side.

They stayed until the bulldozer operator completed the pad for the drilling rig, leveling the ground intuitively, scraping away layers of soil and rock with the ease of long years of practice, until there was a perfectly smooth, perfectly level surface surrounding an obelisk of untouched earth, a red cone surmounted by an immortalized cow chip pierced by a wooden stake.

How could anyone enjoy life as much as Nick did, Dani wondered as she dressed for work the following Thursday. There was nothing feigned about his enjoyment. It was natural and spontaneous and a complete mystery to her. She had never felt that vitally alive, not even before— A spasm of pain stabbed through her and she closed her eyes against it, willing it to leave. Not even before.

She caught her hair back in its knot, but while inserting the hairpins, she paused. Except at the office she had worn her hair loose since Nick had asked her to take it down that first evening. He was taking her to lunch today, a special lunch with Mama Giuseppina of the homemade wine and fantastic salad dressing. *Why not?* she thought defiantly as she raked the pins from the knot and brushed her hair into shining waves. It was becoming progressively harder for her to be both D.J. and Dani. Maybe it was time to begin introducing Dani to the people she worked with.

Dani noticed a couple of inquiring glances, but Marcie was the first to say anything. "If I were you, D.J.," she said thoughtfully, "I'd throw away my hairpins."

The morning passed rapidly—so rapidly that when Marcie stuck her head around the corner to ask if she wanted her to bring her a sandwich, Dani looked up from the abstract she was reading in surprise and shot a startled glance at her watch. Twelve already?

"No," she told Marcie distractedly. "But thanks, anyway. Nick's taking me to lunch today."

"Ah-hah!" Marcie flashed a knowing grin, and Dani felt the blood rising in her cheeks, but by the time she thought of a rejoinder, Marcie was gone and only the echo of her soft laugh remained in the room.

Dani reached for her purse. She considered a trip to the ladies' lounge to repair her makeup but decided against it. Nick ought to be here any minute, and she didn't want to leave him waiting in the empty hall. Using the small mirror in her purse, she touched up her makeup.

She glanced at her watch again. He was a little late, but he hadn't set a definite time. Maybe she'd be able to finish reading the few pages remaining in the abstract she had started.

She finished reading those pages and again glanced at

her watch. Years of habit controlled her. She reached for the microphone of her dictation unit and began transforming the copious notes that covered several pages of a legal pad into sentences and paragraphs. *Where was he?*

When Marcie ducked into the office to tell her she was back from lunch, Dani looked up from her notes.

"Still here?" Marcie questioned.

"Uh—yes." Dani stumbled over her words. "Nick's been... He's going to be a little late." *A little late?* It was one o'clock and she hadn't even heard from him.

By one-thirty, Dani had decided that she must have misunderstood. By two she knew she hadn't misunderstood, but that something must have detained him— car trouble or an accident. By two-thirty, she was furious. He could at least have the decency to call. By three o'clock, when hunger forced her to the employees' lounge to search for an apple, she couldn't meet Marcie's questioning glance. Marcie knew as well as she that there had been no phone call.

There wasn't a piece of fruit to be found in the lounge. Dani located a box of stale crackers in one cabinet and munched one while she let her thoughts run rampant. It was obvious that she had been stood up. Damn him! Did he care so little for her feelings or her schedule that he could just not show up? It was all right for him to disrupt her life, drag her anywhere and everywhere he wanted to go, when he wanted to, but apparently she couldn't count on him.

Count on him? No. She wasn't letting herself be lulled into doing that, was she? "Oh, God, I know better," she moaned. For a moment she saw Rob, smiling and promising, *Forever, Dani.*

She jerked her attention back to the formica counter in front of her, immobilized for a moment, then she crunched the lid into place on the box of crackers and tossed it into the cabinet just as Chet Davis entered the lounge and headed directly for the coffeepot. He paused while pouring his coffee and glanced at her.

"You look very nice today, D.J. You ought to wear your hair down more often."

She mumbled something and all but fled from the lounge. That was another thing! She'd made an absolute fool of herself today, wearing her hair like a teenager, exposing herself to speculation by everyone in the office. If he thought he could treat her with so little regard, then whatever he thought they had going for them was over, finished, through. There would be no more of just what he wanted when he wanted.

What he wants, when he wants! Those had been Marilyn's exact words. Dani stopped in her march down the hall and heard the words again. *What he wants, when he wants.* She had ignored everything the woman said that night, but now she herself was making at least one similar complaint. Should she have listened to Marilyn? *You haven't seen it yet, but Nick does have his darker side,* she had said. Dani shook her head and took another step. *Ask him about the divorce, or better yet, read the file.*

Dani couldn't do that. Not then. Not now. And yet, was there something in the file she ought to know? Yesterday she would have sworn no. This afternoon she wasn't sure. *Nick can be violent. Your only danger will come from him.*

Without stopping to think any further, Dani turned and went back down the hall through which she had just stormed, past the employees' lounge, to the cavernous room that housed central files. She whirled the revolving index to the "S's" and scanned down them until she found the number she needed. With swift competence she located the drawer and extracted the file.

Only when she held the fat, well-used folder in her hands, did she pause. She leaned against the filing cabinets and studied the outside of the folder. The information on the label was scanty—it always was—but the case number told her that the divorce had been filed nine years ago. Nine years. That was a very long time for Marilyn to harbor so much animosity. The sheer size of the folder told her that there had been a lot of activity during the divorce proceedings. Of course, there would have been a lot of arguing over property. Marilyn would have seen to that. There wouldn't have been as much property nine years ago as there was now. Maybe that was part of the reason Marilyn was so upset. Maybe she resented not having waited until Nick had firmly established himself. Dani turned the file in her hand. Maybe—

What am I doing? One clear flash of understanding speared through the morass of her thoughts. *The man is three hours late for a lunch date. That's all! I won't let Marilyn's insinuations—I won't let* myself *make it into anything else.*

Quickly, before she could change her mind, she scribbled a notation on an out card and inserted it in place of the file. She carried the file with her, but instead of returning to her office, she turned at the hallway and went directly to Frank Merriweather's office. His secretary announced her and admitted her immediately.

Frank Merriweather, as usual, missed little. "Is something wrong?" he asked.

Dani handed him the file. "I've checked this out to you. Would you please lock it away somewhere?"

He glanced at the label. "Have you read it?"

"No."

"Do you want to read it?"

"I want you to lock it away. If Nick wants me to know what's in it, he will tell me."

"But you won't ask him?"

"No."

He dropped the file onto his desk and looked into her eyes. "You haven't told him anything about yourself, have you?"

This wasn't supposed to happen! He was supposed to take the file and not question her, certainly not about herself.

"You're going to have to talk about it someday, D.J.," he said patiently, "and if you ever want to have anything lasting with Nick Sanders, you are going to have to tell him."

You're going to have to talk about it someday. Those were the words that had repeatedly invaded the cloak of numbness in which she had wrapped herself for so long, a litany she had grown to hate. *Healing won't come until you do.* Well, healing had come, she had made it come. And without talking about it.

Her glance wavered slightly as she met his probing gray eyes. "I appreciate what you're saying, Mr. Merriweather. I really do. And I know you mean well." She swallowed and tried to calm her hammering heart. "Nick and I are seeing each other. That's all. When, if ever, there is any possibility of developing something 'lasting' with him, then, of course, I'll have to consider telling him.'' She shook her head adamantly. ''But not now. Now it's no more his business than what is in that file is mine.''

''Ask him about it, D.J. It's not as bad as you fear.''

''I can't.''

''Why? Because you're afraid of what you'll learn, or because you're afraid he might question you?''

''Mr. Merriweather...'' Her voice trailed off in a silent plea.

''All right, D.J.,'' he said, sighing. ''I'll keep the file, and I'll keep my unsought advice for a while.''

She tried to smile. ''Thank you.''

''Don't thank me, D.J., until we learn whether I've done the right thing.''

There wasn't much point in remaining in the office—she accomplished nothing—but she did stay, until almost five o'clock when she handed Marcie the title opinion she had dictated earlier.

''There's a reason,'' Marcie said in easy understanding.

Dani smiled grimly, nodded acceptance of Marcie's sympathy and walked quickly down the hallway without answering.

''D.J.!'' Marcie's clear voice cut through the conservative quiet of the offices, stopping Dani at the end of the hall where she had to turn to reach the elevators. Dani whirled around to see her secretary standing in the hallway, the receiver of the telephone in one hand, gesturing wildly. Only one phone call could have made Marcie breach office etiquette by yelling down the hall, and Dani breached it equally badly by running down the hall. She saw Marcie grinning broadly as she turned the corner into her office and grabbed for the telephone. Breathless, frightened, angry and relieved, she pushed the button with the blinking light to answer the call. "Hello?"

Nick's voice crackled over the line, muffled by the intermittent roar of an unidentifiable noise. "Dani? I'm glad I caught you before you left the office." There was a rumble and a strange whooshing sound. "I'm sorry about lunch." But his next words were lost to her.

"Where are you?" She practically yelled, sensing that he wouldn't be able to hear her any better than she could hear him.

"I'm at a truck stop about fifteen miles from the drill site," he yelled back. "We've had trouble with the rig. I've been out here since nine this morning, and this is the first chance I've had to get to a phone."

"You're not drilling already, are you?" she called into the strange noises that floated over the phone wire.

"I told you we were going to drill an oil well," he yelled back and even with the poor connection she could hear the teasing chuckle in his voice. "But I've been up to my neck in mud and grease all day. If you promise not to throw something at me when I finally get there, I'll clean up and take you to dinner any place you want to go."

Dani was laughing when she hung up the telephone and still laughing when she walked out of her office. Marcie stood in her alcove, arms crossed over her chest, facing the doorway and waiting for some word.

"The reason, Marcie," Dani chuckled, "was a cow chip."

Marcie's eyes widened and her mouth dropped open. "A what?"

Dani laughed again and repeated her words as she walked down the hall. "A cow chip."

"D.J.?" Marcie called after her. "Aren't you going to explain that?"

Dani tossed her head, delighting in the feeling of her hair brushing her shoulders. "Nope."

Chapter Seven

It was easy for Nick to persuade her to leave work early the following Friday. Too easy, she thought with a frustrated sigh as she hurried to clear her desk. A smile quirked her lips. But the rewards were worth this little inconvenience. Well worth it.

The thought that she was blatantly carrying on an affair both appalled and intrigued her. It was the sort of thing Rob's mother had always thought her capable of but so alien to her own rigid code of what was right that an occasional stab of remorse pierced through her contentment.

There was a fine line, Dani thought, between loving what someone did for you and loving the person who did it. *God knows I love the things he does for me,* she mused. She loved the excitement he brought into her life. She loved the laughter he helped her to share with him. She loved the small courtesies he showed her, such as plumping her pillow and bringing her coffee in bed. She loved the way he brought her body to life, coaxing it to heights she had never dreamed possible.

Stop that! she told herself. What she was feeling was a natural reaction. Never in her life had she been pampered and petted, and if Nick chose to do so for a short while she would enjoy it, and she would not feel guilty.

She removed the tape from her dictation unit, clipped it into the folder, gathered up her purse and the stack of files, and walked to Marcie's cubicle.

Marcie sat at the typewriter, earphones from her transcription unit clutched in her fist as she stared at the wall.

"Marcie?"

The woman turned toward her with a small shake. "Sorry, D.J. Guess I was lost in thought."

Marcie's face was drawn, and her eyes were unnaturally dull. Dani studied her with a frown. "Are you all right? Maybe you're the one who ought to be leaving early."

"Don't be silly," Marcie said, but her grin didn't light her face the way it usually did. "Your taking off a half day is almost as good as giving me time off."

Dani wasn't convinced, but she smiled at the woman. "Just don't push yourself too hard, Marcie."

"I don't, remember?"

Dani remembered. She remembered the conversation she had had with Marcie days before, and belatedly, she also remembered that the woman's annual evaluation was still sitting on Chet's desk waiting for her signature.

As she took the stairs down to the fifteenth floor, she chided herself for being so wrapped up in her own thoughts she had let something so significant as Marcie's annual raise slide into the background. What else had she let slide? As she opened the door to Chet's outer office, she was still taking herself to task. Her personal feelings must not interfere with her work. Work was the constant factor in her life. It had sustained her before, and it would sustain her again.

"Good morning, Miss Simms." The young woman who spoke pleasantly looked familiar, but her sleek new hairstyle and the artfully applied makeup that emphasized her luminous gray eyes made such a striking difference in her appearance that Dani wondered for a moment if it could be the same person.

"Robyn?"

Robyn laughed and self-consciously patted her hair. "I couldn't believe it either when I first looked in the mirror. It still amazes me."

"It's stunning," Dani told her, noting the glow of her cheeks and the sparkle in her eyes that no makeup could have caused.

"Thank you. Mr. Davis had an early lunch appointment today so he's already left the office. Can I help you with something?"

Dani explained why she was there. Robyn efficiently produced Marcie's file from the banks of now organized personnel files lining one wall and handed the evaluation to her. Dani glanced over it before signing it and handing it back to Robyn.

She's in love, Dani thought as she watched the soft glow on Robyn's face as she separated the copies and sorted them for distribution. Too bad for Chet. If Robyn's looks were any indication, the new boyfriend would have no trouble at all dragging her off to Glenpool or Broken Arrow or anywhere else he wanted. Dani felt a catch in her throat and mumbled her thanks as she all but fled from the room. How long had it been since she had been that young, that innocent, that full of hope?

It was a beautiful, crisp May morning, but as Dani stood in the cavernous underground area of the parking garage waiting for her car to be brought down to her, surrounded by the smell of gasoline fumes, the echoes of car horns and the rumble of vehicles moving above her, she gave in to the gloom and isolation of her surroundings.

Impatiently she glanced at her watch. She had almost two hours to wait before Nick would pick her up, and suddenly she wanted to see him so badly the two-hour wait seemed interminable. Forget the fact that she had wanted to tidy the apartment before he arrived. Forget the fact that she had planned a lingering soak in the tub. Forget anything except at this moment she needed the reassurance of his smile and the comfort of his presence.

When the parking attendant screeched her car to a stop, she waited only until he slid from the seat before jumping into the car. He had barely cleared the door before she shifted the car into gear and shot forward into the light.

Thank God, the street was free from traffic. *Dumb!* she thought. *Get yourself together. You are a rational, adult, professional person. You don't squeal your tires like an adolescent. You don't drive onto a busy street without looking.* A bitter laugh choked her. *You don't run to your lover in the middle of the day.*

But she knew where he was.

Hanging steel, he had called it. "You have to experience it," he had told her only the night before. "There's an exhilaration that can't be explained, watching the girders going up, seeing the building you planned taking shape from a pile of metal." His eyes sparkled while he spoke and his hands moved in restless gestures. "There's only one thing more exciting," he said, "and that's standing on the floor of a drilling rig with the bit pounding into the earth as you reach total depth and knowing you've made a well."

He had turned to her, and she had melted at the look in his eyes as he took her into his arms. "Except maybe... There is one thing more exciting than either of those," he had murmured against her throat. And then there had been no more need for words.

She saw the building across the gently rolling, rapidly developing landscape long before she reached it. It wasn't a small building, unless compared to the Brady Center Towers. Ten stories high, it would dwarf neighboring buildings along the Interstate Highway for a while. Twin cranes perched predatorily over it, and a cluster of trucks and sheds and trailers nested in its shadow.

She missed the first exit and had a chance to view the structure from the height of an overpass. Nick didn't believe in building square cubes, she thought as she noted the as yet indefinable angles jutting out from a central core.

She took the next exit and backtracked to the construction site, parking some distance from the building beside Nick's blue Mercedes. His fair-weather car. Her spirits lifted as she realized he had planned for this to be a fair weather day.

Sand slithered into her pumps as she walked toward the site. A burly construction man in jeans, a yellow hard hat, and a blue workshirt with sleeves rolled up to expose a massive tattoo on an equally massive biceps stopped her approach.

He wasn't impolite, just definite, and she had no trouble hearing his voice over the noise of groaning engines.

"This is a hard-hat area, lady. You can't go any farther. You got business here?"

"Nick Sanders," she shouted back at him over the roar.

He shook his head, grinned, and jerked a thumb in the direction of the roof, or what would be the roof, of the building. Then Dani understood the groaning of the engines. One crane had hooked onto an enormous steel beam and was levering it toward the sky. On the beam, his khaki-clad legs spread slightly and flexed for balance, holding onto the supporting cable with only one hand, stood Nick. He faced the steel shell as he rose with the beam, but she knew by the set of his shoulders, the tapered waist, the sheer size of him— What did it matter how she recognized him? She knew it was he. And she felt nausea rising within her as he grew smaller against the sky.

"Oh, God," she murmured. One slip of the cable, one gust of strong wind, one faltering beat of the engine near her... She clasped her hand over her mouth to stifle an outcry and watched in horrified fascination as the beam reached the top of the building and Nick jumped from one precarious perch to another that couldn't have been any more substantial.

"You want I should tell him you're here?" The man's voice finally penetrated her numbed consciousness.

She forced down the bile in her throat. "What?"

"You want I should go up and tell him you're here?"

Dazed, she looked at the pile of construction clutter

at the base of the building, half expecting to see Nick's broken body lying there.

"Lady?" The rough voice drew her back from her thoughts.

"No," she murmured. "No, thank you." She turned and stumbled back to her car.

How could he? The thought raced through her mind, keeping pace with the racing of her heart. Drenched with perspiration by the time she reached her apartment, she tore off her clothes and let the shower beat at her, but even the steaming water pelting against her couldn't slow her thoughts. With odd jerking movements she dressed in the clothes she had planned to wear, and not even knowing she had done it until she finished, she straightened the apartment.

She sank onto the couch to wait for him. How could he? In less than a month he had torn apart her calm, comfortable world, and now he was out prancing on a steel tightrope a hundred feet in the air. She wanted to hate him. She wanted to hit him. She wanted to tie his feet to the ground so there would be no chance of his repeating the foolhardy stunt she had just witnessed.

She glanced bitterly about the apartment. Already it had lost the impersonality she had so carefully maintained. Generous ashtrays were scattered about the three rooms. For Nick. Two comfortable homespun-covered throw pillows for floor sitting rested in the corner. For Nick. Blue ironstone coffee mugs replaced the Spode she had used. For Nick. Two stemmed crystal glasses now waited for the wine he sometimes wanted with dinner. For Nick. A bottle of Glen-whatsits, the scotch he liked with the three syllable name she never could remember, had its own place in the pantry. For Nick! And he was risking his neck in some foolhardy, daredevil stunt for the excitement of it?

She brought her clenched fist against her knee. She was even wearing jeans—jeans, for God's sake!—because he had finally convinced her that they would be more practical for some of the places he liked to go than her silk or linen slacks. And flat-heeled walking shoes, so that she could keep up with his long strides without stumbling. And a gauze blouse, because he had pointed one out and told her with that maddening twinkle in his eyes that he thought she'd look terrific in one—in blue. And he was playing Tarzan the Magnificent with a ton of steel!

"Stop it!" she cried into the room and buried her face in her hands. Fingers raking her scalp, she tried to slow her breathing, her heartbeat, her thoughts. She stretched her hands in front of her. Already they were trembling so badly she couldn't hold them still. If she didn't do something, quickly, she would be a bundle of insensible nerves by the time he got here—if he got here.

She sucked her lungs full of air and held it while she began the exercises. Clench, grip, extend. Her hands responded slowly to the once-familiar routine. She exhaled, breathed deeply, and tried again. Clench, grip, extend. Still they trembled. Clench, grip, extend. It was helping, but not enough, and not fast enough.

She made her way into the kitchen and groped through the pantry. If all else failed, a good stiff dose of Glen-whatsits wouldn't. She fumbled with the lid, trying to unscrew it, until she remembered that this bottle had a cork under the cap. She pulled it free and poured a small amount of the amber liquid into a glass. Not enough, she thought, and added a little more. She tasted the liquid. It was harsh on her throat and the smell gagged her. Determined, she pinched her nose with her fingers and swallowed the contents of the glass in one gulp in much the same manner as she had taken distasteful medicine as a child.

That ought to do it, she thought as she pounded the cork back in and stashed the bottle back in its nook.

She settled herself onto the couch as warmth diffused through her. Her hands still trembled, so for good measure she resumed the exercises, concentrating only on the mechanics of them until she drove all other thoughts from her mind.

A subdued Dani opened the door for Nick at the appointed time and stepped back to let him enter the apartment. With detached awareness she noted the sparkle in his eyes and the flush of excitement on his face, but she had, by now, neatly tucked everything away and refused even to acknowledge the enjoyment he so obviously felt. She turned wordlessly and started toward the couch.

"Wait a minute!" He laughed and grabbed her into his arms, swinging her around before planting a boisterous and jubilant kiss on her mouth. She held herself passive in his arms until she felt him putting her away from him, setting her carefully on the floor. She kept her eyes open, looking squarely into his, and noticed the frown that clouded his face. He captured her head between his hands and bent to her again, but when his mouth claimed hers, it was not to kiss her. It was to taste her, Dani realized in stunned silence. He ran his tongue around her lips, forcing her lips apart and ex-

ploring their soft inner edges, then probing the moist
recesses of her mouth. It was done without passion or
warmth. It was, if anything, a cold and calculated examination.

He pushed away and dropped his arms to his side.
"Scotch," he said flatly.

She turned and walked listlessly to the couch where
she curled into a corner of it and sat silently. Nick sat
on the other end of the couch, equally silent, and
studied her with troubled eyes. The only sound for long
minutes was the persistent drone of a distant lawnmower.

Nick broke the silence with a sigh. "You've closed
yourself off again."

So what if she had? Dani thought resentfully. What
right did this man have to disrupt her life, censure her
behavior, or question her actions?

"The only thing I've ever asked of you is that you
not do this," he continued in the same dull, flat voice.
"And you promised you wouldn't."

"I promised to try," she corrected him in a voice as
emotionless as his.

"What happened, Dani?" Frustration crept into his
question. "What caused it this time?"

She stared at him without blinking for a moment and
then let her gaze play across his familiar face. She no
longer had reason to resent the obvious enjoyment
written on his face. She had effectively erased that enjoyment. She had managed to wipe the smile from his
lips and replace it with a tight slash. She had turned the
merriment in his eyes to puzzled questions that demanded an answer.

And she had promised to try.

"I went to the construction site today," she said in a small voice.

"I didn't know."

"You were busy. On—on the roof."

"You should have waited. I wasn't up there very long. I just rode up to check on the progress and then came right back down."

"How, Nick?" Maybe she hadn't tucked it away far enough after all. She felt her throat tightening.

"How what?"

"How did you come back down?" She couldn't stop now. "You weren't on the roof when I got there. You were 'riding up,' dangling a hundred feet above the ground on a cable." Her voice grew tighter and shriller. She knew it and couldn't do anything about it. "How did you get back down? Did you slide down the cable like a monkey?" She broke off, fought for control, and lost. "Or did you sprout wings and fly?"

The slash of his mouth softened. "You were worried about me?"

She closed her eyes and once again saw the vision of him lying broken at her feet. She spoke into clenched fists held tightly against her mouth. "I was terrified."

"Dani." Warmth returned to his voice, and he moved toward her on the couch. He took her fists in his hands, caressing them with his thumbs. Gently, but insistently, he pulled her from the corner of the couch and into his arms. With one hand he massaged the tight muscles at the back of her neck. With the other he smoothed the hair away from her face.

"I've been riding those things since I was fifteen years old. I wasn't in any danger."

She placed tentative fingers on his cheeks and looked

deeply into his eyes. "Nothing must happen to you, Nick," she said with an urgency she didn't try to hide. "I couldn't stand it if anything happened to you."

Then she was kissing him, kissing him with a desperation born of her fear and her anger and of a nameless need that rose from a hidden depth within her, grinding her mouth into his, pressing her body against him, unable to get enough of the feel of him. Then he took over, pushing her down on the couch, following her and stretching his length along hers, taming her wild assault, soothing her with langorous stroking, exploring and possessing her mouth with infinite gentleness.

A shudder ran through her and she collapsed weakly against the cushions, no longer struggling to hold him to her. He pulled away and gazed down at her, his eyes as gentle as his touch had been.

Suddenly she couldn't look at him. She cast about for something, anything, to focus on and concentrated on a spot on the ceiling.

"I'm sorry," she said brokenly.

"I'm not," he said with a shaky chuckle. He kissed the corner of her left eye. "I loved it." He kissed the corner of her right eye and then buried his face against her throat and kissed the place where her pulse jumped madly. "I love you," he whispered when he lifted his head.

She lay immobile beneath him and felt herself being drawn into the depths of his eyes. Could he love her? No. If he really knew her, he couldn't. If he knew about all those months, if he knew about...about... She moved her head in protest, but of what she didn't know. He ran his fingers through her hair and held her still while he placed a teasingly soft kiss on her lips.

"But we're not going to talk about that now," he said, unwinding his length from the couch and pulling her to her feet. "Come on. I have reservations for lunch."

"Do you want your cheeseburger with onions or without?" he asked as he whipped the little car into a parking space at the drive-in restaurant.

"Reservations?" she asked dryly.

"Of course. Didn't you notice that this choice space was waiting for us? With or without?"

"With," she said, and she felt a smile tugging at the corners of her lips.

They sat in companionable silence and watched sparrows busily building nests in the colorful corrugated metal awning overhead. Easy music from the radio blended with and muted traffic noises, and the warm May breeze kept exhaust fumes from the passing vehicles at bay.

When the food arrived, he pulled his briefcase from the backseat and placed it between them, covering it with paper napkins and arranging the sandwiches and the cardboard boats of onion rings and french fries on the improvised table.

He bit hungrily into his sandwich. "There's nothing quite like a Number Four with cheese," he said appreciatively. "Except maybe a hot dog from that little place downtown."

"Or maybe your 'cheap imitation' eggs Benedict?" she prompted, laughing. "How do you sustain yourself eating as many fast foods as you do?"

"It's easy." He grinned at her. "It's really much simpler keeping track of nutrition since they knocked the seven basic food groups down to four. I have here," he pointed to his sandwich, "a serving from the meat group, a serving from the cereal group, and a serving from the fruit and vegetable group. And here," he took a long drink from his strawberry malt, "a serving from the dairy group. What more could I ask for? And besides, I don't always have time to stop for anything more substantial."

"Still, you do occasionally need real food," she said, laughing and reaching for an onion ring just as he did. Their fingers met. Playfully, he pushed her hand away and held the onion ring up to her mouth.

"I have an idea," he said. She hesitated, looking at the onion ring and then at him from under a quizzically cocked brow.

"Go ahead." He chuckled. "Take a bite."

Only when she had bitten off a bite of the proffered morsel and started to swallow did he continue. "Marry me. That way you can make sure that I'm properly fed."

The food lodged in her throat. She stared at him wildly and saw that in spite of his lightly spoken words he studied her intently. She grabbed for her lemonade and swallowed deeply, searching for words.

"That's hardly a reason for marriage," she said finally.

"Need a better reason, do I?" he asked lightly, still studying her. "I don't suppose you'd consider just moving in with me—"

"Nick!"

"No. I didn't think so. Are you through with that?" He pointed to her forgotten sandwich. When she nodded, he tore bits from the crust and tossed them to the waiting sparrows. "It will have to be marriage, then. Your bed is comfortable, but it's about six inches too short. The only way I can see to avoid terminal backache is to take you home with me."

She looked at him in dismay, shaking her head, not knowing whether she wanted to laugh or to cry.

"Still not good enough?" he asked. When she didn't answer, he went on. "I guess I could try guilt. How about—you've had your way with me and now it's time to make an honest man of me?"

His tone teased, and yet—and yet, something told her he was hiding behind that tone, knowing how fast she would run from a formal proposal. Still, his light attitude gave her a graceful way out of a difficult refusal.

"Sorry," she said, giving him a mock grimace. "But you know how us liberated women are."

"Too bad," he said, grinning.

Thank God, she thought. *He's going to play along as though it really were a game.*

"I would have made it worth your while too." He gathered up the remnants of lunch and stashed them on the waiting tray.

"Oh?" She laughed outright at his exaggerated disappointment. "Just what had you planned to offer me?"

"Why, a baby and a new pair of shoes every year. What else?"

She choked and then took another deep swallow of her lemonade. "Every year?"

"You're right," he said as he started the car and backed from the parking place. "That is too much. You wouldn't need that many shoes."

He glided the Mercedes skillfully onto the Interstate Highway and drove toward the heart of town, but when they drew even with the skyline of the business district, he eased into the left lane and soon they were speeding toward the west, away from the city.

"Where are you taking me?" she asked, suddenly suspicious.

"It's a surprise."

"Nick! Be serious. Where are you taking me?"

He turned to her with a grin. "I'm taking you to meet my family."

Her smile faded. "Your family? But you told me they live on the West Coast."

"They do. They came in late last night." He seemed not to notice the edge of panic in her voice. "They're at my place on Keystone, but only for one day. My brother's got to get back to L.A. for an arbitration hearing. I told Tim he shouldn't have checked in with his office until he was ready to go home, but he already had. You know how you lawyers are."

"Your brother is an attorney?" she asked in a small voice as she played for time to quieten her tumultuous thoughts.

"Labor law. He's pretty good too. Too good. Now I'll never get him to move back here. And Mom insists on being near her grandson." He gave a delighted laugh. "I wonder if she's gotten Timmie into dancing school yet? Janice would go along with it. She and Mom are on the same wavelength. None of that feuding in-law business there."

He reached for her hand and clasped it. Dani's hand felt numb in his. She stared blindly at the passing scenery. Why was he taking her to meet his family? They'd only known each other a few weeks. He had no business thrusting her into the middle of a family reunion. They would all know that she had no right to be there.

"You'll like my mother," Nick told her. "She's a little old-fashioned, but that's the worst thing I can say about her."

Dani closed her eyes and shrank back against the seat. Rob's words floated around her. *I wish you'd try harder to like my mother. I know the two of you would get along if you'd just work at it.* And she had worked at it. She had tried to please that woman for eleven years, only to have—only to have—

Dani was unable to push back the memory of her last meeting with Rob's mother. It overpowered her, driving away everything else, even the comfort of Nick's hand on hers. She could see her as plainly as though she stood before her now. She had awakened in a blur of pain to see those eyes that were so like Rob's and yet so different, staring emotionlessly at her. Mrs. Simms's voice, clipped and forever haughty, cut through the lingering haze of the medication.

"Well, Danielle, I trust that you are satisfied now that you have succeeded in depriving me of everything I treasured."

Dani's bandaged hands fluttered helplessly and her numbed senses reacted to the cruelty of the words. She felt the weakness of moisture gathering in her eyes and slipping over her cheeks.

"Tears, Danielle? You have no right to tears. You have no right to life. But I do have one consolation. You're more alone than I, and every day you live you'll remember that it's your fault. You have no one to blame but yourself."

"No," Dani whimpered, and then felt Nick's hand squeezing hers.

"What did you say?"

She returned the pressure of his hand, needing his touch. She shaped her features into what she hoped resembled a smile before turning to him. "Nothing," she murmured.

Chapter Eight

Despite Nick's reassurances, Dani remained uneasy about the impending visit with his family. Nick's "place" on Lake Keystone didn't help her uneasiness either. She had expected an isolated rustic cabin at best, but when Nick turned off the highway at an unmarked road she needed no sign to tell her that they were entering Key Point, an exclusive residential community built on a peninsula jutting into the lake.

The iron gates stood open, but Nick stopped to greet the uniformed security guard.

The guard tipped his hat, exposing grizzled hair, and then spoke to Nick with a gravelly twang. "Sure is good to have you all back. Will you be staying long?"

"Not this time, Jake," Nick told him. "You and Hattie will have the run of the place again after tomorrow."

Nick drove slowly along the narrow, tree-lined road, past clusters of starkly modern cedar and glass condominiums that fit, oddly, with the boulder strewn and oak-covered hilltop. The road curved sinuously, now passing widely spaced, expensively rustic homes.

Nick stopped the car to allow a covey of quail to

scurry across the roadway to a meadow on the left.
Dani leaned back against the seat and exhaled tightly
held breath. She breathed deeply, enjoying the dappled
play of sunlight through the leaves. She could hear the
lap of water against land, but the foliage toward the lake
was so lush she caught only glimpses of silvered sunlight reflected from the water's surface.

"It's beautiful here," she said and found herself
smiling with genuine pleasure as the serenity of the discreetly gentled wilderness began soothing her taut
nerves.

"That's better," Nick told her as he caressed her
cheek. His touch, and the warmth in his expression,
completed the soothing process. After all, she realized,
Nick wouldn't deliberately throw her into a situation
where she would be uncomfortable.

She caught his hand and held it to her cheek, placing
a light kiss on it where it touched her lips.

"Christians one, lions nothing?" he asked with a
perception which caused her to look at him sharply before succumbing to an embarrassed laugh.

"That's a little better score than was running through
my mind earlier," she admitted. "But there aren't any
games scheduled for today, are there?"

"No," he said, moving his hand to trace the outline
of her lips, "however, maybe later we can come up
with an enjoyable alternative."

She grinned at him then, half wishing they could skip
the afternoon he had planned and proceed immediately
with his enjoyable alternative.

"You'd better stop that," she said a little breathlessly
as she pulled away from his touch, "or by the time I

meet your mother I won't even be able to remember my name."

"Right," he said, not moving away. "Best behavior for Mother." And all of her uneasiness was back, hammering at the wall of her chest, trying to get out. "Hey," he murmured. "Don't look so stricken." He placed a light kiss on her mouth, pausing for one delicious moment to nibble at her lower lip. "Just be yourself. They're going to love you."

Nick eased the car into gear, and Dani leaned back against the leather seat and watched his hands on the steering wheel as he guided the car over the now completely tree-lined road, wishing that she could be as relaxed and confident about this meeting as he appeared to be.

When the road seemed to curve back upon itself, Nick turned to the right, onto a lane almost hidden by the roadside foliage. A small cabin sat nestled in the woods a short distance from the road. She looked at him questioningly.

He shook his head. "Guest cottage," he said. "Hattie and Jake live in it now and look after the place." He nodded toward the right. "That road leads down to the garage and then on down to the boathouse."

"Boathouse?" she asked. "And guest cottage? Nick, just what kind of *place* do you have out here?"

"You're about to find out," he said, grinning. "We're here."

The road ended in a graveled circle drive in front of a cedar-roofed red stone house protected by two towering blue spruce trees.

It was really rather a modest house, considering its

location. At least that was what she thought until Nick opened one of the double entry doors and she stepped into a terrazzo-tiled hallway.

They stood in an area overlooking an enormous room. The hall stretched away on either side of them, but Dani's attention was drawn and held by the angular glass walls that rose at least twenty-five feet from floor to ceiling on the far side of the room over which she looked and which seemed to thrust out from the hillside and hang poised over the lake itself.

To the left she could see the massive white dam that had impounded the water and created this lake, and beyond that, in the distance, the skyline of Tulsa. To the right, no trace of civilization marred the tranquillity of water and wooded shore.

She hesitated, entranced, until Nick took her by the arm and led her down the wide stairs. Downstairs she was able, for the first time, to draw her gaze from the spectacular view and see the room.

Muted oriental rugs on the polished stone floor defined conversation areas furnished with the chintz and Chippendale Nick had once mentioned and accented by the chrome and glass he had talked of in the same sentence. It was a curious mixture of old and new, starkly modern with comfortably traditional, and yet the blending was so harmonious that no single element seemed to dominate, except, of course, the magnificent view.

She was holding her breath again. She'd have to learn to stop that. Too many things about Nick had caused that reaction.

"This is not exactly a vacation cottage," she said finally.

"No. I meant it for my home."

She heard the quiet pride in his voice and saw the softening of his expression as he glanced about the room.

"But you don't live here." It was not a question.

He turned his attention to her and studied her eyes. "No."

"How can you bear to leave it?" she asked without thinking. If she had a home like this, nothing could keep her from living in it. No. That wasn't so, she realized. She closed her eyes against the sudden pain and then opened them quickly as the knowledge that she had made herself vulnerable to questions flooded through her.

"What is it, Dani?" His voice, his eyes, his hand reaching to clasp her arm all demanded an answer.

"Nothing," she said. It sounded brittle even to her. She gave a defiant toss of her head as though that would make her answer truthful. "Nothing." She smiled up at him. "Don't you think we'd better find your family?"

She could tell that he wasn't satisfied with her answer, but he didn't press her for another. She saw the slight frown that crossed his face before he schooled his features into a smile. "That shouldn't be too difficult," he said as he glanced at his watch. "Mother and Janice are probably in the kitchen."

"Are they on a schedule?" she asked.

"A demanding one," he told her with exaggerated seriousness.

He led the way down a long hall, past a dining room filled with graceful mahogany and paused at a swinging door as though listening. He nodded. "Just as I thought." He put his fingers to her lips, in a gesture warning her to be silent. He eased the door open and they slipped inside.

Across the spacious kitchen two women sat in a blue-gingham-curtained breakfast area, engrossed in the flickering picture from a portable television. Nick stood quietly watching them, a gentle smile playing across his features.

Nick's mother, for that was who she had to be, looked nothing like Dani had pictured. A tiny woman, with short gray hair cut in a casual style, she seemed completely relaxed as she leaned back in the Windsor chair, sipping coffee and dividing her attention between the television screen and the golden woman to her right.

And Janice, for Dani knew that was who she must be, was golden—golden tan and golden hair—dressed in coral shorts and a matching tank top that emphasized the warm glow of her skin and the shapely length of her legs. She lounged unaffectedly in her chair, as equally engrossed in the televised story as the older woman.

Nick waited until music from the set swelled to a crescendo and the announcer's voice began a commercial before speaking.

"Is this all the welcome I'm going to get," he asked gruffly, "after driving out here to see you two?"

"Nick!" His mother rose from her chair as she turned toward his voice. She hesitated when she saw Dani and then hurried toward her son, her progress slowed by a slight limp, but smiling broadly as she crossed the room. Nick met her halfway, lifting her off her feet and holding her against his chest in a great hug. Janice joined them and took her turn at being clasped against Nick's chest. He set her away from him and motioned to Dani.

"Come over here." He laughed. "Mom, Janice, this is Dani."

Dani, once again unsure of her welcome, smiled tentatively at the two women. Nick's mother seemed almost as unsure as she, she thought. The older woman's eyes held a question, but only for a moment, and then she smiled. "Hello, Dani."

"Hello, Dani?" Janice interrupted, laughing. "Is that the best you can do?" A head taller than Dani, she seemed to envelop her when she draped her arm over Dani's shoulder. "Welcome to the zoo," she said cheerfully. "And if you can still tolerate that brother-in-law of mine after an afternoon of putting up with his family, you're better than he deserves."

Janice's warmth was contagious. Dani felt herself being drawn to it. She could feel the affection flowing among the persons in the room. They were truly a family, she realized, separated by distance and divergent interests and yet united by some bond she had never known. Her throat tightened, and she felt a tiny flicker of anger—no, it couldn't be anger—for what she had missed.

Playfully Nick pushed Janice aside and draped his own arm over Dani's shoulder, drawing her close to his side.

"Speaking of family," he drawled, "where is the rest of it?"

"Fishing," Nick's mother said.

"And whatever you do," Janice added, "don't distract Tim too much. Otherwise, we'll have to have steak at our fish fry tonight."

In the soft eruption of laughter, in the confusion of loving rejoinders that sparked from one to the other, Dani felt herself welcomed into the closely knit group. The feeling was alien to her, yet delightfully comforting, and she pushed back her last, lingering uncertainties and allowed herself to accept the affection that seemed so freely offered.

Nick's mother hurried to get extra cups and soon they were all seated at the round, dark pine kitchen table as Nick regaled them with tales of the Brady Center dedication and the tribulations of drilling the Cow Chip Number One, which, if one believed his stories, must be resembling a Marx Brothers' film.

"How on earth did you come up with a name like that?" Janice sputtered.

"Ask Dani," Nick said, grinning wickedly.

Janice turned to Dani expectantly, but Dani flushed and became suddenly interested in studying the pattern on the stoneware mug she held. "Oh, no," she said softly. "I refuse to take any more responsibility for that well than I already have."

Nick's laugh rang through the room, and he hugged her closer to his side. "Dani staked the well," he told Janice and his mother.

Thoroughly embarrassed, Dani searched for a topic of conversation not related to her. "Have you ever seen a location built?" she asked. "It's fascinating the way the bulldozer operator leveled the ground just by looking at it and deciding where to make his cuts. I would have thought he'd need levels or sextants or at least stakes, but he just *did* it." A thought lodged and she pursued it. "Nick, what will happen to that location after you finish drilling? Will you seed it with grass, or will you just leave it raw?"

"Are you still worrying about that poor overgrazed pasture?" he asked indulgently.

"Yes," she admitted.

"Dani almost took me to task about the surface owner's neglect of the property," he explained. "I think if she had her way, all my locations would have irrigated, manicured lawns and picket fences with climbing roses on them."

"Well?" Dani said indignantly.

He laughed softly. "I'll reseed the location regardless of what happens, but if we make the well I'm hoping for, you just tell me what color to paint the fence and what color roses to plant."

"Enough!" Mrs. Sanders said, holding her side and attempting to regain some composure. "You two go find the boys."

"What is it, Mom?" Nick teased. "Time for your show?"

Janice went off into another fit of laughter before confirming his suspicions. "She's missed it three days in a row, Nick."

In the flurry of laughter and parting comments, Nick opened a many-windowed door and guided Dani out onto the stone breakfast terrace and on down the meandering stone steps.

She sighed contentedly and slipped her arm around his waist. How foolish of her to have been frightened of this meeting. She leaned close to him, reassured by her welcome.

"Nick?" she murmured.

"What?" He rubbed his hand up and down her arm, drawing her closer to him. She could hear the lap of water plainly now, combined with bird calls and the stirring of leaves above her.

"You're a lot like your mother," she said. "But she's so small. Do you take after your father?"

His hand tightened convulsively on her arm. "I look like him," he said in a voice devoid of laughter. "That's all."

What had she said to trigger such a change in him? She started to pull away from him, to look up at his face, when Janice's voice interrupted.

"Send Timmie to the house, will you?" she called from the terrace. "He won't like it, but it's time for his nap."

Nick waved in agreement and turned to Dani with a sad half smile that seemed to plead for understanding. "My father died when I was twelve," he said. "It took me years to sort out the way I felt about it. Sometimes, even now, I have trouble accepting my feelings."

"Which are?" Dani asked softly, his need causing her to break her own rule of not asking anything that would lead him to think he had the right to question her.

Nick half turned from her, thrust his hands into the hip pockets of his jeans and stood staring over the now visible lake. He spoke softly, but firmly. "That it was the best thing that ever happened to this family."

He looked back at her, studying her for any reaction. A thousand questions hammered at her, but she could voice none of them—she had asked too much already. He stood so still, waiting—waiting for her to condemn his thoughts? Ridicule his feelings? She could never do that. Silently she went to him and slipped her arms around him, resting her head on his chest. She wasn't sure whether she was comforting the man Nick had become, or the defiant little boy he had been, but she knew that one, or both, needed comfort.

She held him until she felt him draw a deep breath

and then she turned her face to his. He crushed her to him as his mouth descended. They clung together, taking from each other, giving to each other the comfort each needed. At least, in that precious moment, that was how it seemed to Dani, that while Nick had no way of knowing her hidden pain, he shared his strength with her while drawing on hers.

"Hey! Are you two going to stand there necking all day?" This time the voice, a masculine one, came from below them. "Or are you going to help me catch dinner?"

They pulled away from each other reluctantly, and Nick grinned lopsidedly at her before calling down toward the lake. "No! And no!"

"Just what does that mean?" the voice called back.

Nick took her hand and hurried her down the remaining steps. A younger, shorter version of Nick waited for them at the bottom. Dani watched as the two men embraced, and then she was hauled into a bear hug by the waiting man.

"You're Tim," she said when he released her.

"How'd you know?" he said, grinning.

"Lucky guess." She laughed.

There was the sound of running footsteps from the dock and a blur as a whirlwind passed her and hurled itself at Nick. "Uncle Nick! Uncle Nick!"

Nick caught the boy and swirled him aloft. Dani watched in amazement, her head swirling almost as fast as the young boy. My goodness, but they were a *touching* family, embracing, hugging, reaching out to pat one another—so different from the sterile, emotionless couples who had raised her.

The boy, again on his own feet, tossed back the dark

brown hair from his forehead and glanced at her obliquely with hazel eyes before advancing on her, his hand outstretched. "I'm Timothy Daniel Sanders, Jr. I'm seven years old and I live in Los Angeles, California. Who are you?"

Dani choked back a laugh and matched his seriousness, extending her hand. "I'm Dani Simms—"

"Danny?" he interrupted before she could decide just how much more information he would require. "I thought you were going to be a boy. I don't suppose you'll be playing baseball with us now, will you?"

Dani had to smile as Nick swooped down on the boy and turned him toward the house. "That's almost the same reaction I had when I met her, Timmie," he said, chuckling, "but, no, she won't be playing baseball with us now, and we won't be playing baseball now, because your mother wants you at the house now."

Timmie looked up at him in disgust. "Nap?"

Nick nodded seriously.

"I guess if I stayed you'd just talk grown-up talk anyway, wouldn't you?"

Nick nodded again.

"In that case, I'll humor her." He trudged up the first few steps. "But not for very long. I'll be back real quick for baseball."

Dani waited until he was out of hearing range before letting her laughter bubble forth. "He's only seven?"

Tim joined her laughter. "He was born a little old man. Sometimes he plays at being a kid just to keep up appearances, but he never really convinces us. Come on. I've got a cooler of beer over here and some extra fishing tackle.

Dani politely refused the offer of fishing tackle but

accepted the cold beer as she settled onto the end of the fishing dock and let her legs dangle over the water. Nick sat down beside her, between her and his brother, and popped the top on his can of beer.

"Aren't you going to help?" Tim asked Nick.

"Nope. Told you I wouldn't," Nick said as he sipped his beer.

"You mean you're going to make me catch the whole dinner?"

"You wouldn't want me to spoil your reputation as a mighty hunter by catching more fish than you, would you?" Nick teased. "Go ahead. You can impress the women today with your prowess. I'm just going to enjoy myself."

They joked back and forth for several minutes before Tim invited Dani into the conversation.

"Where did you take your degree?" he asked.

"Oklahoma City University," she said before thinking.

"Night school?"

"Yes."

"That's a hard way to go," Tim said sympathetically.

"It was the only way I could go," Dani answered, not letting herself reflect too long on the years of working and going to school and... She took a long drink from the can she held.

"I hear that," Tim told her. "If it hadn't been for big brother's checkbook, I'd have had to do the same thing."

Tim reached into the cooler and drew out another beer, offering it to Dani. She shook her head, but he insisted. "One more won't hurt."

She handed him her empty can and took the cold

one. "I haven't done this since college," she said, sighing as she leaned back against a piling.

Tim offered another beer to Nick, who shook his head in refusal. Tim shrugged, opened the can for himself, and tossed the empties into a paper sack. They clinked as they hit other cans in the sack, and Dani noticed Nick's frown. Just then Tim's fishing line began whizzing and all their attention was drawn to the struggle he had to land his catch.

"That's it!" he said triumphantly as he managed to net the fish.

"You don't expect to feed us all with that one minnow, do you?" Nick asked in a drawl. "I'm not sure it's even big enough to keep."

"What are you talking about? It's two pounds if it's an ounce." Tim glared at Nick, but his eyes sparkled. He pulled a stringer of fish from the water and added the latest one to it. "Do you think this will be enough?" he asked gleefully.

"How many of those did Timmie catch?" Nick asked, still not apparently impressed.

"Four," Tim said and exploded into laughter. "I don't suppose you're going to help clean them either, are you?"

When Nick grinned and shook his head, Tim said, "I didn't think so, but it was worth a try. The outboard's operational if you want to go for a ride."

Tim left, still chuckling, and Nick moved closer to Dani, taking the untouched beer from her, draining its contents into the lake, tossing the empty can into the sack, and gathering her into his arms. "Do you want to go for a ride? I know a wonderful little cove," he said, nibbling at her cheek, "where we can have marvelous, absolute privacy."

Dani felt tendrils of delicious sensation uncurling in her stomach as she leaned toward him, turning to catch his tantalizing lips with her own. "But you came out here to be with your family," she murmured against his mouth.

"Mmmm," he said before silencing her.

Nothing existed for Dani but Nick as they hovered suspended between water and sky. She felt the sun warmed boards of the pier beneath her as he eased her down onto it, but only in contrast to the warmth of his body pressing against her and the heat she felt growing within herself. She moved closer, fitting their bodies more perfectly together, frustrated by the scraps of cloth that separated them, lost in the wonder of the sensations he never failed to evoke in her until, somehow, realization of where they were penetrated her drugged mind and she began drawing away from him. He protested, holding her more firmly, as his lips trailed temptingly from her mouth to her ear.

"Nick," she moaned, barely able to speak. "Best behavior for Mother."

"Right," he murmured as his mouth found the open throat of her blouse.

"Nick." She inched away from him, breathing heavily, wanting nothing more than to be able to continue. "Best behavior for Mother."

"Right," he said as his mouth again claimed hers, silencing her protests in a slow, resistance-destroying kiss.

"How do you breathe?"

Dani tore her mouth from Nick's and jerked her head toward the unexpected voice. Crouched on the pier, studying them intently, sat Timmie.

Her gaze flew to Nick's startled eyes, and she felt the blood rising to her cheeks.

"Is it really more fun than baseball?" Timmie asked.

Nick grinned at her sheepishly and then helped her to her feet. She stumbled against him, and he held her for a moment before ruffling the little boy's hair. "You'll know the answer to both of those questions soon enough, brat."

Nick's casual attitude, and the boy's acceptance of his answer, helped calm Dani's racing pulse as she tried to remember just how involved they had been and what the boy could have seen.

"Grown-ups sure kiss a lot," the boy said, shaking his head. "Mom and Dad do it all the time now."

"Do they really?" Nick asked. As Dani watched a satisfied smile break across his face, she rid herself of the residue of her embarrassment. It was obvious that Timmie had not been aware of the simmering undercurrents taking place on the pier.

"Timmie!" Tim's voice called from the top of the steps.

"Got to go now. I got out of my nap, but now I've got to clean the fish I caught. Dad just sent me down for the cooler."

As quickly as it had appeared, Nick's smile was replaced with a scowl. "Tell your Dad I'll bring the cooler," he said. "You go ahead and get started on those fish."

Dani declined Timmie's offer to teach her how to clean fish and joined Mrs. Sanders and Janice in the kitchen. There, to her surprise, the afternoon flew by as the three of them worked in harmony, shredding cabbage for slaw, preparing and assembling the ingredients for a hot German potato salad, and consuming gallons of coffee while they visited with the ease of old friends. When the men brought the fish, now transformed into fillets, into the kitchen, Nick's mother took her place at the stove, and Dani and Janice carried the food to the dining room and set the long mahogany table, gently chiding Nick and Tim for forcing them to spend the afternoon slaving over a hot stove. Nick's mother interrupted their spirited repartee when she arrived with the platters of golden fish and hush puppies, but only for a moment.

Dani was caught completely off guard when, once seated, the entire family sat with bowed heads while the older Mrs. Sanders said a brief prayer of thanksgiving.

Dani raised her head to find Nick grinning at her. Completely out of character with the past few moments, he winked broadly and then said in a voice loud enough to be heard around the table, "That's the last of the civilities. You'd better dig in if you want to get anything to eat, but watch out for flying forks."

"Nicholas!" his mother said in a shocked voice. "You'll have Dani thinking we're a bunch of savages."

Why, she's worried about what I'll think of her! The knowledge stunned Dani. She obviously wasn't the only one who had been concerned about this meeting, but for Nick's mother to be worried about what *she* would think...

She caught the older woman's troubled gaze. "Oh, no," she said, trying for the same light tone that had carried them through the afternoon. "I know that Nick has been properly housebroken"—she shot a wicked glance at him—"even if he sometimes acts as though he hasn't been."

The conversation flew around the table as the food was passed and consumed, and Dani joined in the light bantering as though it were something she were accustomed to. Only one thing marred the perfection of the meal, but perhaps if she hadn't been watching Nick so closely she wouldn't have seen his frequent frowning glances toward his brother. Tim, unlike the rest of them, had vetoed the idea of iced tea for a beverage and throughout the meal he managed to down a quantity of chilled white wine.

When the last hush puppy was finished, and Nick and Tim lighted cigarettes, Mrs. Sanders and Janice stood and began clearing the table. Dani rose to help them, but Mrs. Sanders stopped her.

"No, dear. You've done enough today. You go on into the den with the boys."

Janice joined her protest. "Everybody gets one time to be company with this family. Take advantage of it. Besides, you don't want to do Timmie out of his turn with the kitchen chores, do you?"

Nick hugged Dani against him. "Not if it means he won't be properly housebroken."

The room lay in darkness except for soft light from two discreet lamps. Dani caught her breath at the view of the skyline at night. She wandered contentedly to the wall of glass, Nick's arm securely about her, and leaned against him in silent communication as they watched the millions of artificial stars twinkling in the distance.

Dimly she heard Tim moving at the other end of the room, but for now she and Nick were alone. She looked up at him and found him watching her, all traces of harshness erased from the planes of his face.

The glow in his eyes warmed as she smiled up at him in appreciation for his gift of a perfect day.

"Share this with me, Dani."

And in those words she realized the answer to longings she had not dared to acknowledge. She turned in his arms and this time she did not try to hide, even from herself, the anguish that she had for so long pushed back.

"It's not that I don't want to," she whispered, "but too much has happened...too much."

"Whatever—" he began, but he broke off as Tim approached them. She pulled away and turned to Tim, to silence Nick, she admitted to herself. She forced a smile for Nick's brother which turned to one of genuine amusement as she watched him trying to juggle three filled glasses.

Tim held his hands toward Nick. "Your scotch and water is the front one," he said. When Nick took the glass, Tim gestured toward a stemmed glass. "I didn't know what you wanted, Dani, but Janice swears by this cream sherry."

Following Tim's lead, the three of them walked across the room. Dani sank onto a low sofa, and Nick settled himself beside her, while Tim took a wing chair facing them.

Somehow the conversation turned to a discussion of the differences between the two fields of law which they practiced, with Dani attempting to explain how she felt about the exactness of title law, and Tim arguing for the excitement the human element added to labor law. Nick sipped his drink while he watched the interchange between them, and Dani, after one taste, only held hers, but Tim drank steadily. As the level in

Tim's glass grew lower, the frown on Nick's face grew deeper.

When Tim finally emptied the glass and started purposefully across the room with it, Nick's voice erupted from him in a low roar. "Just where in hell do you think you're going?"

Dani, who had been watching his darkening mood, still did not expect the heat of his words. Tim, who had apparently not noticed anything to foreshadow Nick's reaction, was clearly stunned.

"To get another drink, Nick," he said calmly. "Why?"

"Why?" The words came out too clipped, too controlled. "Because you have been drinking steadily since before I got here this afternoon. That's why. Don't you think you've had enough?"

Tim turned to face Nick, and a look of disgust twisted his handsome features. "Listen, big brother. I haven't had a day off in over a year. I finally got a vacation and now I have to cut it short after one day. I'm home—or rather I'm the closest thing to home we still have back here—and enjoying myself, and if you don't like the way I do it, I'm sorry, but I don't think your letting us spend the night in your house gives you the right to come down on me like that."

"Tim, I'm not coming down on you. I'm concerned." Nick seemed completely unaware of Dani as he spoke to his brother. "I know what this can do. Your marriage is back on an even keel. Don't risk it. My God, you've even got Timmie fetching beer for you, just like—"

Tim's words interrupted him. "Just like the old man. That's it, isn't it, Nick? Everything boils down to that.

Well, let me tell you something. I'm not the old man, and neither are you, and I don't see you swearing off alcohol.''

"I don't have a problem," Nick said coldly.

"Neither do I, big brother, neither do I. I don't spend every dime I make on booze with the boys, I don't get so damned drunk I beat my family, and I'm not about to kill myself or cripple my wife by running my car off a bridge. I had enough of that when I was growing up. I'm not about to repeat it, and I don't need you to be my self-appointed keeper to make sure that I don't.''

Soft laughter from the hallway announced the arrival of the others. The two brothers glared at each other in silence for a moment before Tim turned away and marched across the room. Nick sank back beside her. Dani twisted the stem of the wineglass between her fingers, studying it to avoid staring at Mrs. Sanders's limp. Now the reason for the pain in Nick's earlier words was startlingly clear, and she wished, almost, that she had not heard the answer to her unspoken why. How had he survived a childhood like that? Hers had been lonely, but any abuse she had suffered had been from neglect, not violence. Sensing the tension still gripping Nick, she slipped her hand into his, and he clutched it, squeezing it until her fingers grew numb.

Janice seemed aware of the tension, but she attempted to cover it as she set a tray on the low table in front of the sofa and began dispensing coffee. Timmie bounced on the couch beside Nick, and Mrs. Sanders dropped into the second wing chair with a sigh of contentment.

"A perfect day," Mrs. Sanders said. "I just wish we had more time here."

"You're welcome to stay, Mom. All of you are. You don't have to leave just because Tim has to go back to work."

"Oh, no," Janice said as she accepted a glass of sherry from Tim and settled herself on the arm of his chair, draping her arm over his shoulder as he sat beside her. "Whither thou goest, and all that stuff."

An uneasy silence fell over the room, and Dani wished for a diversion, any diversion. She felt Nick's arm around her shoulder, but she held herself erect, not giving in to her need to lean on him. Tim, at last, provided the diversion, and even while he spoke, the words of a familiar cliché rang in her ears. Be careful what you ask for, the saying went. You might get it.

Tim was obviously casting about for anything to smooth over the silence. He began talking about arbitrations he had participated in years before, when he was just beginning to establish himself.

"Your name has sounded familiar to me all day," he said as he warmed to the story, "and I've finally remembered why. There was a dockworker's strike in Oklahoma City. All flights out were cancelled because of snow, and Janice was at least nine and a half months pregnant. I didn't want to be there; we weren't any closer to a settlement than the day I arrived, and I couldn't have left even if we had been. There was a nice young man there, a union representative for the employees. He took me off to one side during a break and finally got me to admit what was bothering me and calmed me down so that I could at least listen to what was being said in the hearings. He had a son, about a year old..."

No! Dani thought. *It couldn't be. Please, God, don't let him say it.*

"... beautiful little boy, blond hair, blue eyes. His name was Simms, too. Do you know him?"

He'd said it. He'd asked. And there could be no doubt who he meant. How like Rob it would have been—to pull out the picture and proudly show off his son. How like him to have given comfort to a stranger. But why, God? Why this stranger? She could always deny... No! She could no more deny him now than he could ever have denied her or their son. She turned toward Nick. He shouldn't have to learn this way, and yet, now, there was no other way. She caught his glance and saw only polite curiosity mirrored there. She felt the easy grip of his hand on her arm.

"Probably not," Tim went on. "It's a big city. I can't remember his first name—"

"Rob," Dani said, her gaze never leaving Nick's eyes. "He was my husband."

She saw the polite curiosity turn to shock and felt the easy grip on her arm bear down painfully.

"Oh..." Tim was speechless for a moment, but the silence was heavier than before. "Sorry about that, Dani," he murmured. "Cute kid, though," he said, as though grasping at anything rather than leave the room in its deathly quiet.

Don't, please don't, she moaned inwardly, all the time watching Nick's eyes.

"He's about eight now, isn't he? I wish we'd known about him," Tim went on innocently wreaking destruction. "He and Timmie would have had a good time together. Where is he today?"

The shock in Nick's eyes had given way to questioning, and then to—what? Revulsion? It was a hard way for him to learn that she had once had a family, but to what conclusion had he jumped to make him look at her with *that* look?

His hand gripped her arm mercilessly. "Yes, Dani," he said in a deceptively soft voice, "just where is he today?"

Suddenly it was more than she could bear. She had never talked about it with anyone, and to do so now, with people who were once again strangers, to do so now with Nick, who looked at her with eyes glinting dangerously from chiseled impassive features, she couldn't—she couldn't.

She took a deep breath and said as evenly as she could, "Bobby is with his father."

Chapter Nine

Nick didn't pause long enough to put the top on the Mercedes. She'd been aware of his making his excuses—they must have been adequate because she vaguely remembered the smiles of his family as they had bid them good-bye. He had released his punishing hold on her arm only while embracing the others and then had resumed his grip. She knew he had practically dragged her up the stairs, but she hoped no one else did. She knew that he had pushed her into the car seat as though he could no longer bear to touch her.

The night air was cold—colder than it had any right to be after the warmth of the afternoon, and the open car, racing along the divided highway as though its driver were pursued, drew the chill air inside and wrapped it around her.

Dani welcomed the chill as she sat huddled against the car door, for its discomfort kept her from thoughts—thoughts that swirled around her, as they had so often in her nightmares, thoughts that threatened to overpower her, to drag her back into that world of darkness and pain.

She felt her hands clenching and knew that now not

even that familiar deception would work for her. Nick
would notice, if he ever looked at her again, which
didn't seem too likely at this moment, and he would
have one more question for her. He clutched the steering wheel as though it were his safety line. And the
tension in his hands was matched by that in his jaw. He
could have been cut from stone except for the vein
pounding near his temple, visible even in the dim light
cast by passing cars.

Hadn't she known, though, since she let him into
her life, that this time would come. Yes! And yet,
somehow, she had begun to think that when the time
came, if the time ever really came when she would
have to tell him, she would be able to tell him only that
which she was able to bear, and he would look at her
with the understanding which he had shown her in the
past, not pressing her to delve too deeply into what had
happened, and why.

Maybe he wouldn't press her, she thought as she
looked at his expressionless profile. Maybe he would
simply let her out at her apartment and disappear from
her life. She could tell that he had already drawn conclusions as to why her son wasn't with her. Could those
conclusions, wrong as they had to be, be any worse
than the truth?

The truth. What was the truth anymore? What had it
ever been? She could no longer bear to look at Nick.
She turned her unseeing eyes toward the approaching
lights of Tulsa. Bobby was with his father. That much
was true.

She raised her eyes toward the real stars, the ones
overhead. Oh, God. It was coming again, and this time
she couldn't stop it. She had no more power over it

now than she had in her sleep. Less. Sometimes she was able to awaken herself to end the dream, but she was already awake and it was starting anyway.

It always began as this afternoon had been—happy. Happy. And then— She sank back against the seat as the familiar scenario began unreeling, forever captured by her memory as though on film, and she was the unwilling audience of one, destined to live through it again and again and again.

It always started the same, with her spluttering in surprise—could she still be surprised after all this time—and grabbing the piece of old towel from her jeans pocket and scrubbing at her nose. "You—you..."

Don't fight it, she told herself. *It won't do any good, anymore to fight it.*

"Picasso, I think," Rob had said as he held the paintbrush upright between them and focused with it. "It's a perfect match for your eyes."

And then Bobby had joined in, gurgling with laughter. "Mommy's blue. Mommy's blue."

And Dani was caught, trapped forever in that moment of time. In her memory she eased herself onto the edge of the bathtub, repeating the movement as she had countless times in her dreams, and surrendered to the inevitable, as that day she had surrendered to her laughter. After all, she had thought then, what would a little more paint hurt. It had dripped off the ceiling and splashed off the walls all that morning. Her work jeans were completely ruined, as was her frayed flannel shirt, and her long strawberry blond hair had streaks of blue running through it, but her fellows weren't in any better shape.

Her fellows. Warmth enveloped her as she watched

them. At three, Bobby already showed promise of having his father's good looks, but when she looked at him, she saw only innocence in his cotton white hair and cornflower eyes. When she looked at Rob, her breath caught in her throat. Four years of marriage had only intensified the rush of longing she felt when she saw his slender body, hardened by hours spent on the loading dock, or gazed into his compelling blue eyes.

She had shaken herself back to the task at hand. "I've changed my mind," she told Rob. "We aren't painters, you know. I think we should have left this for the next tenant."

"Not on your life," Rob swore. "You may have already taken the bar exam, but I still have one more semester to go, which means at least six more months in this trap. Besides, you've always wanted a blue bathroom, and for you, m'dear," he gestured with both hands toward the pale blue ceiling, "the sky is the limit."

She smiled at him. "Robert Simms, I don't know how I ever got along without you."

"Ah, shucks, Dani," he drawled, "don't get mushy in front of the kid." He leered at her suggestively and twirled an imaginary mustache. "Any chance we can send him to a sitter this afternoon?"

"Lech," she hissed at him. "Come here, Bobby. You've got blue on you, too."

She twisted around to the bathtub and dampened a cloth under the faucet, frowning slightly as the ancient gas water heater in the corner growled to life. She wiped down the squirming boy before looking back toward her husband.

"No chance for a sitter," she said in a mock whisper

as she rose to stand beside him. "But I can put him down for a nap right after lunch."

Rob slipped his free hand around her and squeezed her against him. "Then what are you waiting for, woman. Food is in order."

"Yes, Master," she said, planting a kiss on his cheek. "Come on, Bobby. Help Mother with lunch."

"Want to stay with Daddy," the child protested.

She cocked an eyebrow at Rob. "It will be quicker."

He grinned. "Okay, Bobby, you stay with Daddy, and when we get this piece of wall and the door done, we'll go help Mommy together."

She ruffled her son's hair and reached automatically for the cigarettes and lighter sitting on the end of the tub. No. She changed her mind. She was smoking too much. She'd leave them where they were until after lunch.

She felt a little light-headed as she walked into the living room. Strange, she didn't feel ill, but these moments of weakness seemed to be coming regularly.

She opened the front door. The early April air still carried a reminder of winter, but the house needed airing. She breathed deeply of the fresh air and felt better. Leaving the door open, she crossed into the kitchen and began preparing lunch. Something easy, she decided. And quick, she added with a grin.

She glanced around her contentedly. Rob called the house a trap. In no way could it be compared with the home he had known all his life, but she didn't see it as a trap. A duplex unit among a cluster of closely spaced duplexes, it was infinitely better than student housing, and with Rob's weekend carpentry work, her coordinated curtains and slipcovers and the books and records and things they loved scattered around, they had managed to make it a real home. "Rather a cozy nest," she said aloud as she checked the soup and popped the sandwiches under the broiler.

"Are you two about through in there?" she called. "Lunch in five minutes."

"We'll be there," Rob's voice sounded muffled, and it lowered slightly as he spoke to his son. "Bobby, put that down. That's Mommy's."

She grinned as she turned to the sink. Breakfast dishes soaked in now cold water. She turned the hot water tap on them and reached for clean plates in the cabinet above.

The explosion shook the dishes in front of her hand. She looked at them, not comprehending, for a split second, until she heard her son screaming, "Mommy! Mommy!"

"Rob?" she called, but there was no answer from him, just Bobby's high-pitched wail of agony.

She whirled and ran toward the bathroom, screaming Rob's name. The door was closed. Why was the door closed?

She twisted the knob and pushed against it, but it wouldn't budge. "Rob!" she screamed. "Bobby!" No answer came from inside the room, only a strange, ominous crackling that she refused to identify.

Something wedged the door shut. She could feel it near the floor. She heard voices behind her, but nothing mattered except getting the door open. She put her shoulder against it and felt it give slightly. She slid her hands into the small opening and pushed with all her strength. The flames shot out at her, searing her hands, igniting her hair.

Someone grabbed her, pulling her away from the door and jerking her shirt over her head, but the only sound she heard was that of her own scream going on and on and on.

"You're home."

Dani slumped back in the seat. Through the windshield she could see the facade of the apartment building. Laughter from the playground in the next courtyard drifted to her on the night breeze. Familiar scenes, familiar sounds, they were now strangely unreal, more a dream than her dream.

Reluctantly she dragged her head around toward the accusation she heard in Nick's voice. He stood beside the door, holding the door open.

"You have to get out. You can't sit there all night." He did not offer her his hand then or when she started up the sidewalk. She heard the car door slam and felt his unyielding presence beside her. She couldn't reach out to him. He wouldn't reach out to her.

At her apartment she turned to tell him—good night? Good-bye? Which was it to be? And did it really matter now? All she wanted to do was close her door on the world, curl up in a tight ball on the end of her couch, and wait for this night to be over. And it would pass. The sun would come up on a new day, and she would begin her routine as though none of this had happened. But why—why couldn't tomorrow be Monday instead of Saturday? On Monday she would have had the pressures of the office to count on. On Saturday she would have only herself.

And why wasn't Nick leaving? Why was he just standing there, looking down on her?

The kitten bounded from the shrubbery and began insinuating itself around her ankles, purring loudly as he did so, and Dani felt her tightly held control beginning to fray. Blindly she fumbled for her key. Nick took the keys from her, opened the door, and walked into the apartment. The kitten entered, too, going directly to the kitchen, mewing loudly. Dani stood alone at the door, outside, not wanting to go in, having no other place to go. She watched Nick follow the kitten into the kitchen, and she watched him as he took a bowl from the cabinet and got the milk from the refrigerator. She might as well not be there for all the attention Nick was paying to her, and yet she had no doubt that once she entered, he would turn on her with questions and deny her the solitude she so desperately needed. Evicted. Effectively evicted from her own home. For, impersonal though it was, the apartment was the only home she had.

It was too much! She stepped into the apartment and found words for the first time since leaving Key Point. They grated in her throat as she hurled them tightly across the room.

"That cat does not belong in this house."

Nick glanced at her and continued pouring milk into the bowl. "The cat isn't the issue, Dani," he said in a voice as tight as her own.

"Get him out of here."

Nick picked up the cat and the bowl of milk and carried them to the front door. He straightened, closing the door.

"And you go with him!"

His hands tightened on the door before he closed it completely, locked it, and turned to face her.

"No. If I leave now, we'll never get this resolved. If I leave now, any hope we had for something together will be gone."

"If that's a threat, you've made a serious error, Nick. I won't be pushed into anything by an ultimatum."

He leaned against the door, his palms spread flat against the wood on each side of him. "That's not a threat, Dani, and it's not an ultimatum. It's a statement of fact. I can't leave you alone to pull that wonderful little trick of yours of shutting out the rest of the world, of shutting out me, until I know just what in the hell has happened."

He ran his hands through his hair, and for a moment he looked tired and defeated. He shook his head. "I want to see his picture."

"Picture?" Dani repeated incoherently.

"Photograph. Snapshot. Portrait. I want to see a picture of the son you never once mentioned. I want to see what he looks like. I want to see if he looks like you. I want to try to get some idea of why you haven't even hinted at his existence."

Dani steeled herself. It was worse, much worse than she had feared. Nothing had prepared her for this reaction from Nick. Where was the compassionate, understanding friend she had known? Where was the gentle, considerate lover who had soothed and comforted her? He glared at her from across the room, and she returned his baleful look, hearing the sound of her own heart roaring in her ears.

A picture? He wanted to see a picture of Bobby? *So did she!* Too bad, Nick Sanders, she thought even as she spat the words at him. "I don't have one."

"Oh, hell!" He strode to the desk and yanked open a drawer, rifling through the contents with both hands.

"What are you doing?" she cried.

"I don't believe you."

"Nick, don't do this." She ran to his side and tugged at his arm, trying to stop his search. "Please don't do this."

He shrugged away from her touch and yanked open another drawer. "I'm going to see that picture whether you want me to or not."

"I don't have one!" she screamed at him. Oh, God, why couldn't he believe her?

He pushed past her and went into the bedroom. She heard him pulling open drawers in there and followed him as far as the door. If possible, his face became even harsher as he opened each of the bureau drawers, finding nothing but her neatly folded clothes. He seemed to falter when he found the article featuring him, but he tossed the newspaper back in place and slammed the drawer. He opened the closet door, felt along the shelf, looked beneath the clothes, and even opened her one suitcase.

When he came out of the closet, he sagged against the door frame. "Where do you live?" he asked in a voice devoid of emotion.

Was it over? Or was it just beginning? At least he was no longer raging at her. "I live here," she said in a small voice.

"No. You keep your clothes here. You sleep here and eat here and bathe here, but you don't live here. There's not one sign of you in this apartment—not one thing that makes this place uniquely yours. Not one thing that tells me who you are, or why you are, or *what* you are."

He gestured about the room. "This isn't a home. It's little better, if any, than a hotel room." He shook his head. "You've stayed here for four and a half years, and yet if you walked out of here tomorrow, with the exception of maybe a few clothes, you wouldn't miss a damned thing, would you?"

No! She wouldn't miss one damned thing. Not ever again. And she'd never miss one damned person. Not ever again.

"Where are you, Dani?" He stood close to her now, so close, and yet separated from her by so much.

Where was she? *Where was she?* A laugh tore itself from her throat and in escaping sounded suspiciously like a strangled sob. She let her gaze be drawn to the bathroom door and then closed her eyes as a quick, violent shudder moved through her.

He misunderstood. Of course, he misunderstood. There were two drawers in the bathroom. Dani huddled against the bedroom wall and listened to the noises as Nick searched those drawers.

Should she tell him about the fire? It would be so simple just to say, calmly and rationally, that she had lost her husband and son in a house fire. But could she tell him that and not tell him the rest of it? Would he let her stop there? She clenched her hands into fists as she waited for his return. Damn him! What right did he have to demand answers from her.? And what made her think that she had to give him the answers?

"What are these?" Nick held the prescription bottle in his outstretched hand.

Dani slumped against the wall with a sigh. She was not strong enough to fight with him any longer. Whatever they'd had together, if ever they'd really had anything, was ruined. The truth couldn't make matters worse. She'd answer the questions she could bear to answer, and when she could no longer bear it, she just wouldn't say anymore.

She looked dully at the prescription bottle and spoke in a low monotone. "I used to take them to help me sleep."

"*Help* you sleep? Don't you mean knock you out?"

She turned her head from him in defeat, resting her cheek against the wall. "If you already knew what they were, why did you ask?"

He threw the pill bottle across the room and grabbed her shoulders in his hands. "Because I want you to tell me what has happened to you that makes you have to drug yourself into unconsciousness to sleep. Where is your son, Dani?"

"Oh, Nick." The words trembled on the tip of her tongue, crying to be said. *He's dead.*

Nick didn't give her time to say them. His fingers bit into her shoulders as he shook her. "Where is he, Dani? Did you do something so horrible his father took him from you? Or was it just too much trouble to be a career woman and a mother at the same time?"

His eyes glittered in the harsh light of the room. "Or was it alcohol, Dani? For someone who once told me you didn't drink, you've been doing your share of it lately. Did I start something up again by forcing wine on you that first night?"

She tried to back away from him, but the wall held her. "What kind of person do you think I am?" she cried.

"I don't know any longer," he muttered. He looked at her, but she could tell he wasn't seeing her. "But I've got to find out. What did you do to your son?"

He'd never understand. Dani knew in that instant that she would never be able to explain to this half-crazed stranger who looked at her with eyes glazed with something that couldn't be pain. Could this be the same man who had held her so tenderly that magical night at the fountain lifetimes before? His words from that night echoed through her mind and then hung heavily between them as she realized she had repeated them aloud. "I promise I won't pry into areas you don't want me to know about."

His mouth twisted with what at any other time she would have thought self-mockery, but now she knew that any mockery was directed at her.

"You have a selective memory." His words grated harshly in the silence of the room. "Don't you remember the rest of it?" His grip tightened on her. "Don't you, Dani? Don't you remember promising not to close yourself off from me?"

Now whose memory was selective? She tried to ignore the pain he was causing her, the pain in her shoulders, and the other, within her, that was twisting viciously around what had been her heart. She looked directly into his eyes and for less than a second wondered about the bitterness she saw there before her own bitterness overcame her and she spat the words at him. "I promised to try."

"And are you?" he demanded.

She closed her eyes against the probing intensity of his gaze and felt—oh, no, not now—felt herself beginning to tremble. She fought it, as she always fought it, willing herself not to give in to this weakness, but soon the wall and Nick's hands were her only strength.

"That's another handy little trick you have." His

words cut through her veil of concentration. "Guaranteed to garner sympathy from the most hardened adversary, isn't it?" He spoke carefully, shaking her to reinforce each word. "Well, it's not going to work this time."

"Why, Nick?" she screamed at him. "Why are you doing this?"

His mouth twisted in a grimace. "Because I loved you, Dani. And, God help me," he groaned as he jerked her against him, "I still want you."

His kiss was meant to punish her, meant to exorcise her from his life, and knowing that, she endured the ravishment of his mouth. But when she felt a tremor course through him, when she felt him moan against her throat, and when she felt his hands become, not gentle, but less violent as they moved over her, she recognized in his actions something she was all too familiar with. She recognized despair. She recognized anguish. How ironic that she could cause those feelings in someone who, until tonight, had given her nothing but happiness—who had given her the only happiness she had known in five years.

Oh, Nick! The realization cut through her. *I never meant to hurt you!*

When his mouth again captured hers, she met his harshness with tenderness, parting her lips and accepting the aggressive thrust of his tongue. She slipped her arms around him, holding him to her, as though she could draw his pain from him and absorb it with her own.

With her response she felt a change in him. His hands suspended their violent trespass and slid to her back, holding her arched against him. His mouth ceased its plunder, softened and moved persuasively over hers. She felt a deep sigh move through him as, after long moments, he dragged his mouth from hers. He looked down at her as though she were someone he had known a long time before but couldn't now quite recognize. "God help us both," he muttered thickly as he lifted her in his arms and carried her to the bed.

He undressed her efficiently, and she lay passive as he did so, searching his face for some trace of the gentle lover she had known. When her clothes lay in scattered piles about the room, he stood looking down at her, then crossed to the light switch and plunged the room into darkness. She heard the soft rustle of his clothing as it joined hers. She felt the slide of his skin against hers as he stretched his length beside her and gathered her to him.

She had thought only to provide a haven for him, to comfort the hurt she felt in him, knowing all the while that too much had happened for her to be able to take pleasure from the act of love. But her body, her deceptive, traitorous body again betrayed her. It had grown too accustomed to the pleasures Nick brought it. Even while her mind denied her ability to respond, Nick's tongue and lips and fingers sparked that impossible response to life, until she was moving against him, matching him caress for caress—not just to give him comfort, but because she loved the taste of him in her mouth, the feel of his skin on her fingers. And when they joined, desperately it seemed to her, her mind was still refusing to acknowledge her response, still refusing to accept the possibility of fulfillment, while the sensations in her body took her ever upward, finally drawing her into an ascending spiral of feeling where her mind could not follow.

Nick was with her, moving with her, guiding her upward, urging her with an intensity she had not dreamed possible toward the blinding light waiting for them at the top of the spiral. Never before had she been this high. All the other plateaus they had passed—mountains they had seemed at the time, seemed so very far below, and still they climbed until the light surrounded them, shattering behind her closed lids. His name caught in her throat and then tore from her in a long cry as she shattered with the light and collapsed against him drawing long shuddering breaths which matched his.

They lay locked together, breathing raggedly, until Nick smoothed her hair away from her face and drew her into the crook of his arm, nestling her head on his chest. He said nothing. She was incapable of forming words.

She felt the thud of his heart beneath her cheek, and the rapid rise and fall of his chest until his breath steadied, even as hers steadied, and she sank into peaceful lethargy. Then her mind caught up with her. It didn't say much, and yet it said everything. It repeated Nick's words so clearly that had she not known by his even breathing that it was not so she would have sworn he spoke them again. *I loved you, Dani. And, God help me, I still want you.*

Loved. Past tense. Want. Present tense. The significance of his words drove away all lethargy and left her chilled. Well, she argued with herself, wasn't that what I wanted? She had told herself she didn't want him to love her. She had told herself that all she wanted from him—a moan escaped from her when she realized how naive she had been—that all she wanted from him was a physical relationship. She had wanted more, much more, but even then she hadn't had a prayer of ever truly having it.

Nick sighed and drew her closer. Be careful what you ask for. That was the second time the half-forgotten saying had popped into her mind that evening. But she had certainly gotten what she asked for. The hollowness of her victory mocked her, and Nick's still moist body pressing against her became a burden she could no longer tolerate. She eased away from him, intending to rise and go into the other room, but he stirred when she moved. As though one arm were not enough to hold her to him, he threw his other arm over her and burrowed his face against her throat, his body echoing the tension she felt. To try to move now would rouse him, and Dani was not able, yet, to face the questions she knew had only been postponed.

She lay rigid within the prison of his arms, staring at the pale blur of the ceiling for what seemed like hours until at last the stress of the day claimed its toil and she sank into troubled sleep.

She knew she was dreaming. She knew it the moment she saw the dishwater. And she knew just as quickly that something was wrong. The dream never started in the kitchen. It always started in the bathroom. The scenario never changed, and yet here she was, staring at the breakfast dishes. She knew what she must do, but something kept her from it. She pushed against the force that held her, shook free of it, turned on the hot water tap and reached for the dishes in the cabinet. She saw them shaking on the shelf and heard Bobby screaming for her. Although she opened her mouth to cry out to Rob, no sound came from her throat, and when she turned to run for the bathroom the same restraints as earlier kept her from moving. She struggled wildly against them until she was free. She still could not find her voice, but she felt the carpet beneath her feet as she dragged her way to the bathroom door. It refused to open. She threw herself against it with a sob, pounding on it. She could hear the noises behind it, crackling and then roaring. She forced the knob, found the small hold for her fingers, put her weight against it, pushing to dislodge the obstruction that held it closed, sobbing an incoherent prayer as she collapsed on her knees on the floor in the midst of flames that could never again sear her, and this time the high-pitched wail she heard came from her own throat.

Hands drew her away from the flames, lifting her from the floor. A mouth covered hers, cutting off her cry. Hands soothed her hair and held her in a protective embrace.

"Dani, what is it?" Nick's voice cut through the shadows of the dream. He held her, just outside the bathroom door. "For God's sake, what is it?"

She shook away from him and looked up at him, dazed. She felt a hollowness behind her eyes and knew that it would signal tears, if she were able to cry. *Tears, Danielle?* Rob's mother seemed to be with her, as she had been with her those first days at the hospital, as she would always be with her, looking down on her with ice blue eyes. *You have no right to tears. You have no right to life.*

"Tell me, Dani," Nick insisted, reaching for her. "What is behind that door?"

Why had she even thought she could love again? Why had she even thought she had the right to try?

She shrugged away from Nick's tentative hand on her arm, reached in the closet and got her robe. She belted it around her and then went carefully about the room, picking up his clothes and his shoes. She brought them to him and held them toward him.

"What are you doing?" he asked.

There was no emotion in her voice when she spoke, because she no longer felt anything. She walked, she breathed, she could even speak, but there was no life in her. She knew that now. "What you told me long ago I should have done," she said evenly. "I want you to get the hell out of my life."

He started to speak, but something in her eyes must have silenced him. He took the clothes from her. She went into the living room and huddled on the couch while he dressed. She saw nothing. That was the trick, she had learned during those long months. To see nothing. Not the things that were there, but more importantly, the things that were not there.

A hand rested lightly on her shoulder. They were still doing it. After all this time, they still hadn't learned that she didn't want to be summoned for meals, or to go through the motions of physical therapy, or to sit across the desk from the doctor and have him tell her, again, that her feelings were a natural reaction to what had happened.

The hand moved down her arm. They never went away. She might as well do whatever it was they wanted this time. It was the only way they would leave her in peace. She dragged her head around to face the intruder. It was not a nurse.

Nick knelt beside her, filling her vision. Was that compassion she saw in his eyes? She didn't want compassion from him. She wanted what she had known from the first that she could never keep. She wanted what he had offered and she had destroyed.

She turned her head so that she could no longer see him and, inevitably, felt his hand slide from her arm. She heard the click of the front door being unlocked and felt the soft rush of air as it was opened. She heard the sound of his footsteps as he moved from the carpet to the concrete of the porch.

Still she stared blindly at the wall opposite her. He'd left in such a hurry he hadn't even bothered to close the door. She'd have to get up and do that. In a little while...

Chapter Ten

"Damn it, Dani. I can't just go off and leave you like this." Nick's words came from the doorway.

Her hands clenched convulsively and she knew she was dangerously close to losing the tenuous hold on what control she had left.

He stood outlined against the gray light of early morning, solid and strong, and for one fragile moment she dreamed of throwing herself against him and letting him wrap her in his strength. She couldn't. His concern was for Dani, a person who had existed for a few short days only because he had willed her to and who, tonight, had ceased to be.

But if the Dani he knew no longer existed, why did she feel her throat tightening as she looked up at him. "Please," she whispered. "I don't want you here."

It was as though she hadn't spoken. He closed the door and leaned against it. "We have to talk," he said. "I'm not leaving until I understand what's happened."

God! Why couldn't he just go? Didn't he realize she couldn't take much more?

Too vulnerable curled in the corner of the couch, she felt herself unwinding from her cramped position, rising to her feet, and walking toward the kitchen, putting as much space as possible between herself and Nick's looming form. She turned and stared into the darkened kitchen as she heard her voice, calm and cold, chiseling away at any feeling he might have left for her.

"You had no trouble drawing your own conclusions on the way home from the lake. All you demanded from me was confirmation. Draw your own now and consider them confirmed."

She heard his muffled oath behind her and remained silent, but when she felt his hands on her shoulders her tautly stretched nerves could stand no more. "Take your hands off me!" she screamed, even as a small voice deep within her moaned, *Don't let me do this, Nick. Don't let me say these things. Please, Nick, don't ever let me go.*

He spun her around to face him, his fingers biting into her arms.

"Dani—"

"That's the answer, isn't it, Nick?" Her voice caught and then rose again. "Push me around. Shake me some more. Maybe you could even manage to throw me on the bed again and make mad love to me while you make sure I know that's not what you really want to do!" Wonderful love. Tender love. *Please,* Nick.

"Listen to me!"

She couldn't listen to him, any more than she could listen to herself, for if she did she might hear those words that clawed always at the back of her memory, those words she had so far been able to keep pushed back. And she couldn't look at him, couldn't bear to see his face tightened by the control he was forcing on himself, couldn't bear to see his beautiful green eyes clouded and questioning.

He had to leave! She had to make him want to leave! Now, before she was lost.

"Is this how you handled Marilyn?" She hurled the words at him, hating herself for doing it but grabbing at anything that would push him away.

"Damn Marilyn—"

"Why? Because she wouldn't let you bully her?" Nick, a bully? Never. Only tonight, stretched beyond his limit by things she didn't understand, couldn't stop to understand, had he ever been other than gentle.

A hard, gut-level blow wouldn't have been more effective. She watched his face blanch to an ashen gray. He closed his eyes, but not before she saw the flash of pain that speared through them. He finally released her shoulders, clenching his hands into fists and holding them tightly against his thighs. He took a deep breath and opened his eyes, eyes that were devoid of expression.

"You want to know about Marilyn?" he asked in a voice that matched his eyes. "Let me tell you about her."

"No," Dani whispered. What had she done? If only she could erase that look from his face, hold him to her and tell him she didn't mean what she said. But she couldn't—not if she were to save herself. "No! I don't want to hear about your ex-wife. I don't want to play true confessions. Isn't that where this is leading? You'll tell me your horrible little secret and then I'll tell you mine and throw myself at you begging your forgiveness so you can be kind and gentle and understanding?" *If only she could!*

He pulled her to him, murmuring her name over and over, moving his hands through her hair, across her back, trying to soothe her, she knew, trying to calm her, and she couldn't let him. She forced her hands between them, splaying them against his chest, and pushed free from him. She stood crouched, ready to run, dragging air into her lungs but unable to fill them.

"Do you really want confessions, Nick?" she cried, no longer able to stop. "Do you really want to know where my son is? He's—" The word lodged in her throat. Too long denied, too long unspoken, she would say it now. "My son is dead!" she cried. The word hung between them, palpable and real in the room, but once said, once pushed past her throat, it freed others dammed within her.

"Dead. Dead in the fire that killed his father."

She heard Nick moan, "Oh, my God."

"Dead in the fire that destroyed the pictures you demanded to see." She heard her voice rising, shrill and hard. "Dead in the fire that destroyed the kitchen clutter and the closet clutter you bemoaned." She was screaming at him now. "Dead in the fire that left me scarred, but alive. And I—"

She caught herself in midbreath, stunned into silence. What had she almost said? Abruptly, unexplainably calm, she watched shock and sympathy battle for control of Nick's features.

"And I hate you, Nick Sanders, for making me say that."

She could breathe now, but the air was heavy in her lungs, weighing her down, as the air on her flesh pressed in on her. And she was incredibly weary. She turned from Nick and leaned against the breakfast bar.

"As I hate you for disrupting my life, for giving me an illusion of happiness, for helping me to forget, and then forcing me to remember."

She heard his steps behind her and shrank closer to the counter. "If you must understand something tonight," she continued in a monotone, "understand this. I have nothing else to say to you. Now or ever. And understanding that, you ought to be able, at last, to leave."

Would he reach out to her? He was so close she could feel the warmth of his body. She waited, not breathing, knowing by the prickles of electricity along her flesh that he held his hand poised near her shoulder. But then he was gone, the soft thud of the door the only sound she heard as he left, and she clutched at the counter, its unyielding surface her only support, her only comfort.

The shrill summons of the telephone recalled Dani from the fitful sleep into which she had finally fallen. The first ring jolted her upright in her corner of the couch. On the second ring she identified the sound and started to rise. But it was Saturday, she thought groggily. No one ever called her on Saturday. No one but Nick. The instrument jangled a third time. It wouldn't be Nick. Not after what she had said. A fourth ring. But it might be.

She watched the instrument warily as it rang again. Fool! she chided herself. It's only a telephone. Either answer it or ignore it. But she could do neither. She continued to watch it in hushed suspense until after the twelfth ring it fell silent.

She dragged a hand through her hair and shook her

head as if that would shake off the panic claiming her at the thought of having to talk to Nick again. She smiled grimly. Foolish to worry about something that would never happen. But, just in case, she lifted the receiver from the telephone and lay it carefully on the writing pad of her desk.

Then she went methodically about the apartment, emptying the ashtray Nick had used earlier, smoothing the covers on the bed, removing any trace of his visit. She retrieved her clothes from the floor and hung them in the closet. There was no point in putting them in the laundry now. They would never be worn again.

The prescription bottle lay on the floor where Nick had thrown it. She picked it up and carried it into the bathroom. She looked at it for a long time before removing the lid. How long since she had taken one? Months at least. She had been so proud of not needing that kind of help. She was still proud of it. Why, then, did she keep them? Unless—unless the keeping of them close to her was in itself a dependence. Quickly, defiantly, she upended the bottle over the toilet. She gave a yank to the handle and watched the swirling water carry away what nebulous protection the pills had offered. She tossed the bottle toward the trash, not bothering to watch it land, spun on her heel, and left the room.

That expended her little store of energy. She went through the mechanics of making coffee and carried a blue ironstone mug of it back to the sofa. She curled once again into her corner of the couch, tucking her feet under her.

In a little while, she told herself, she'd get up and do something, anything to occupy her mind. In a little while, but for now—she took a deep breath and leaned her head against the sofa cushion. The smell of Nick teased her senses. The scent of his after-shave and cigarettes had permeated the apartment. In a little while, maybe she would open the windows and air out the apartment. There was work at the office that had to be done, that should have been done Friday. Maybe she'd go downtown and pick up a few files. That had always helped before. Maybe she'd do that. In a little while. But more than a little while passed as she sat huddled and alone on the couch, and her untouched coffee grew cold in the cup.

The first hesitant tap at the door was an irritation Dani decided to ignore, but when the noise persisted, she pushed herself off the sofa. At least it wasn't Nick's bold knock summoning her. It was probably just someone selling magazines, she thought as she reached the door. She opened it to see a fiercely determined Marcie raising her fist to knock again.

"Marcie?"

Marcie's face eased into a hesitant, troubled smile. "I hope you don't mind, D.J. I've been up for hours and I—I had to talk to someone. May I come in?"

Dani swung the door open. "Of course," she said. She watched with a puzzled frown as Marcie crossed to the couch and sat, obviously ill at ease, on the edge of it. Dani realized she still held the cup of now cold coffee so when she closed the door, she walked to the kitchen, dumped the cold coffee and filled the cup with hot coffee and without asking filled the other mug for Marcie.

"What's wrong?" she asked as she set the cup on the table near the woman.

"Nothing," Marcie said quickly, but Dani noticed her catch her lower lip in her teeth and watched a variety of emotions cross her face as the normally open and outspoken woman seemed to edit her thoughts.

"Well, maybe something," Marcie said finally. She gripped her coffee cup and charged into what she had to say. "I'm almost used to Joe being gone during the week—not quite, but almost, but the weekends are ours. They always have been. But he's stuck in Kansas City this weekend, on *my* time, and the house just seemed to close in on me. I guess I got to feeling sorry for myself. I shouldn't have. He's finally gotten his promotion. I'm going to be able to quit work and stay home when the baby is born. And he's promised me that he won't have to travel nearly so much, but—but I just didn't want to be alone. Do you know what I mean?" She asked the last in a small voice.

Dani took a deep breath and leaned back against the sofa. So, she would be leaving after all. "I know exactly what you mean," she confessed with more honesty than she intended.

Marcie was just what she needed, Dani reluctantly admitted to herself later that morning. She was much better for her than house cleaning, or working on office files, or what had been most probable—sitting with numbed mind unaware of time's vacant passage.

By the time they finished the pot of coffee, Marcie had thrown off her glum mood and reverted to the irrepressible imp Dani had come to rely upon.

"You've got to go with me to the flea market," Marcie insisted. And without knowing why she was doing it, Dani gathered clothes and went into the bathroom to dress for shopping at the flea market. She hesitated before stepping into the shower. Her body still bore the subtle imprint of Nick's lovemaking, the feel of him and the lingering scent of him. For one wild moment she longed to hold those sensations to her as long as she could. Instead, she stepped under the spray and lathered every inch of flesh, deliberately and thoroughly.

Marcie drove a tiny foreign economy car with a confidence that bordered on terrifying for Dani, but she did get them to the fairgrounds with nothing more serious happening than one silver-haired man shaking his fist out the window of his car at them as they sped past. They parked almost at the door of the building which housed the weekend flea market.

Once inside the vast exhibit hall, though, Marcie slowed her pace to little more than a crawl. She examined every item in every booth with a thoroughness that both frustrated and intrigued Dani.

"This would be marvelous on your coffee table," Marcie said of an onyx paperweight. Dani didn't think so. And, "Don't you think this is perfect for that corner in your bookcase?" This was asked of an art nouveau statuette of a woman clothed with half a drape and a flower. Dani was trying to think of a tactful rejection of the idea when she noticed Marcie's eyes twinkling with laughter. Sometime just before daylight she had thought she could never laugh again, but now she surprised herself by giving in to a reluctant chuckle.

"No," she said. "But if you want to put her on your counter, *I* won't say anything."

A hot dog and a soft drink at the halfway point sustained them until they finally left the building a full three hours after entering. Marcie's purchases consisted of the onyx paperweight, an earthenware pitcher, and a pair of turquoise earrings.

"But you have to buy something, D.J.," Marcie moaned as she noticed that Dani was empty-handed. "You can't spend that much time with that much wonderful junk and not buy anything. It's—it's un-American!"

"I'll tell you what, Marcie. I'll buy lunch."

"Lunch? Omigosh!"

"What is it?"

"I left this morning without feeding Max and Killer. We have to run by the house before we do anything else."

Dani soon discovered that running by the house was not quite as simple as it sounded. It required a thirty-minute drive to a suburb of Broken Arrow, a small city south of Tulsa. Marcie and Joe lived in a subdivision of new brick homes, some so new the lawns were still scars of raw earth. Marcie's front lawn, however, was green and lush, with neat borders of young shrubs and annual flowers. Marcie led her into the house, through a large living room with a cathedral ceiling and stone fireplace, into the L of the dining room and kitchen. The house was scrupulously clean but had scattered stacks of books and needlework projects lying around what appeared to be Marcie's favored nest. Marcie opened a sliding glass door and stepped out onto the patio. The stockade fenced backyard was divided by a chain link fence. Half the backyard was a vegetable garden. The other half was devoted to dog.

A weimaraner bounded over to jump on Marcie.

"Killer?" Dani asked as she watched the girl disengage the dog's paws from her shoulders.

"No. This is Max." Marcie gave a shrill whistle and

motioned toward the doghouse. A pomeranian peeked from the doorway. "That's Killer."

Somehow the afternoon turned into evening. Marcie always seemed to have just one more thing to do before they left. "Just let me get these few weeds from around the tomatoes. You know how a garden can go to pot if you don't stay right on top of it." And, "Just let me dry one load of clothes. These are going to mildew if I don't get them out of the washer." Then, "It's so late now, why don't I fix us a snack." Eventually, turning on the television, "I've been wanting to see this movie for ages. Would you mind very much if we watched it? It's the last play date."

What is this? Dani wondered. Where was the devastated woman who had knocked on her door that morning practically begging for company? Marcie seemed supremely capable of filling her own time without any help. And yet, wasn't that what Dani was so good at? Who was she to criticize another person's method of doing it? Still, Dani was beginning to feel unneeded, despite Marcie's friendly comments during the day and even during the movie, until Marcie turned off the television and turned to her, hesitant again.

"D.J., would you think I was awful if I asked you to stay the night?" She hurried on before Dani could speak. "By the time I drive you into Tulsa and get back, it will be after midnight, and the house will be empty." Marcie sighed deeply. "And Joe still won't be here."

"Marcie, I hadn't even thought about—"

"If you have other plans, of course I'll take you home."

But Dani could tell that she really didn't want to. "I didn't bring anything with me."

"Oh, that's all right." Marcie rushed to say, "I can

let you have a nightgown, and I buy toothbrushes by the handful. Joe's always losing one when he goes off on a trip.''

Why not? Dani thought. Why force Marcie to drive for over an hour round trip to take her back to emptiness?

Dani shrugged helplessly. "Why not?''

She had changed into the nightgown Marcie provided and was walking down the hall from the bathroom to the guest room when she heard the telephone ring and Marcie's muffled voice when she answered. "No, everything's fine,'' she heard Marcie say softly. "D.J.'s spending the night here.''

It must be Joe, Dani thought, smiling as she slid between crisp, colorful sheets. And then she thought no more because almost as soon as she lay her head on the pillow she was asleep.

Marcie was already up, seated at the table with coffee and the Sunday newspaper, when Dani wandered into the kitchen the following morning.

"Sleep well?'' Marcie asked as she poured coffee and passed it to Dani.

"Like a baby,'' Dani said, amazed at how rested she felt. "And you?'' she asked, remembering Marcie's reason for wanting her to stay.

"Better than I thought I would.''

"Joe's call last night didn't have anything to do with that, did it?'' Dani teased.

"Joe's...'' Marcie's cheeks flushed bright red. She ducked her head and smiled sheepishly. "Have some of the newspaper,'' she said abruptly, passing the front-page section across the table.

Dani took the paper but she didn't look at it. She

looked instead at the comfortable, cozy atmosphere of the rooms around her. She looked through the open drapes at the well-tended garden and the two dogs romping companionably in the backyard. She glanced covertly at Marcie—married to a man she loved and who obviously loved her and soon to have his child. Dani tossed the paper to the table, poured herself another cup of coffee, and carried it to the patio door where she stood looking over the garden. Marcie had been smart to turn down the promotion. A career was a poor substitute for what she had.

"D.J.?"

"Mmmm?" She turned slowly to see Marcie pointing excitedly to an item in the newspaper.

"Mid-South has staked a well in Beckham County, and if I'm not mistaken, it's on that same piece of ground that Sam Wilson tried to peddle to Nick."

Dani took the paper from her and hurriedly scanned the entry. "That slimy weasel," she said under her breath. The man had worked a farm out agreement all right, but not for Nick, for himself. "He wouldn't release Nick's money but he went ahead and peddled his leases before they were released."

"Can he do that?"

"Not ethically," Dani said grimly. "And if Nick should decide to take any of them, Wilson would never be able to sell anything to Mid-South again."

"But if Mid-South has the top leases that take effect so soon, why would they want to buy these?"

"Because of the royalty payments," Dani told her. "The old leases call for an eighth of the proceeds to be paid to the mineral owner, but the new ones specify three-sixteenths. That's half again as much and a bunch of money in a big well." She crumpled the paper in her hand. "When are we supposed to close the escrow?"

"Tuesday," Marcie told her. "At ten."

"Nick ought to know about this," Dani said and then remembered that she wouldn't be the one to tell him. She handed the paper back to Marcie and slumped onto the chair. "Would you call Henry Slayton first thing in the morning? Tell him about this and ask him to be sure Nick knows about it before they meet Tuesday."

"But aren't you going to the bank with him?"

"No," Dani said. "No. He's not my client, and now that Henry has returned from his vacation I'm going to give the files back to him."

It sounded so simple when she said it that way. If only all she had to do to get him out of the rest of her life was to hand a folder over to someone else.

"D.J.?" Marcie's hand on hers dragged her back from her thoughts. "I asked if you were ready for breakfast."

Dani forced herself to concentrate on something as inconsequential as food. "Only if I get to help fix it."

"Okay," Marcie agreed. "You cook the sausage while I mix up the waffles. And fry a little extra. Max and Killer love it."

Max and Killer loved the waffles too, Dani discovered when they took their leftovers out to the dogs. Killer was at a distinct disadvantage because of his size, but he made up for the difference by jumping frantically for the tidbits Marcie held out to him. Max woofed good-naturedly, but it was obvious he wasn't going to let the little dog get more than his share.

"Here," Marcie said, laughing as she handed a waffle to Dani. "You feed Max while I take care of this little monster."

Marcie bent down to pamper the tiny dog while Dani called to Max and held out the waffle, but Max wasn't having anything to do with her. Obviously Killer was getting something special and he wanted a part of it. It happened so fast, Dani didn't realize what was happening until it was over. There was a sharp yap, a short growl, and then Marcie was sprawled on the ground between the two dogs.

"Marcie!" Dani hurried to her side. "Are you hurt?"

"I don't think so," Marcie said shakily. She levered herself up on her elbows and looked at the dogs, now happily roughhousing across the yard. "But I'd better figure out a safer way to feed them. That could be dangerous later on."

"What do you mean later on?" Dani asked. "Here," she reached to help Marcie to her feet, "let me get you into the house. You're going to call your doctor."

"Call my doctor?" Marcie shook her head. "Over a little tumble like that? I've fallen a lot harder and a lot farther and not called a doctor."

"Not while you were pregnant," Dani reminded her. She settled Marcie on the couch, brought her the telephone, and stood over her until she made the call and then insisted that she lie still until the doctor returned the call.

"Well?" Dani asked when Marcie hung up the telephone. "What did he say?"

"He said to take it easy today," Marcie told her, grinning, "and to come into the office at eleven tomor-

row, unless I feel drastically worse before then. And,''
she said pointedly, ''he said not to worry.''

''Right,'' Dani said. She marched into the bedroom
and returned with two pillows and an afghan.

''What are these for?'' Marcie asked. ''He said take
it easy, not go to bed.''

''I don't know of any law that says you can't be comfortable while you take it easy,'' Dani told her, hiding
her anxiety. She tossed the pillows to Marcie. ''Now,
do you want a magazine, a book, your needlework, or
the television?''

''I want to get up and do the breakfast dishes,''
Marcie said.

''That's out of the question. I'm doing the dishes.
You're staying put.''

Marcie's obstinacy threatened to take over, but Dani
stared it down. ''Needlework,'' Marcie relented.

Dani handed her the needlework and went into the
kitchen, around the corner from, and out of sight of
the couch. She wiped viciously at the counter with the
sponge. Marcie had to know how precious the life she
carried was, but did she know how fragile? The doctor
was right—she shouldn't worry, but would she take it
easy if she didn't have someone to insist upon it, and
could she take it easy if she had to drive that tiny car
into Tulsa and back taking Dani home? Dani knew the
answers to those questions. No and no.

She caught herself smiling at the memory of Nick
answering Tim with those same words. She threw the
sponge into the sink and tackled the stack of dishes.
Could she let herself remember the good times?
Maybe later, she decided, when the good times weren't
so interwoven with the others. For now—for now she

would make sure that Marcie stayed down for the day. One more day and night away from the apartment was one more day and night she didn't have to spend alone in it.

When she saw Marcie settled into bed that evening and tucked herself between the sheets in the cheerful guest room, impossibly drowsy, she knew she had done the right thing. The ring of the telephone startled her, but she smiled when it rang only once and then was silent. The soft, muffled voice from the other end of the hall didn't carry words, but Dani didn't need to hear the words. Marcie was loved. That much was evident. For one moment she gave in to the wish that the call had been for her, and then she pounded her pillow, turned over on her side, and closed her eyes.

Nick's face floated behind her closed lids, haunted, stricken, hurt. She opened her eyes wide, holding them open against the new image. It was impossible to close her eyes and not see him.

"Oh, Nick," she moaned into the softness of her pillow.

Chapter Eleven

"What do you mean, not go to work this morning?" Marcie asked indignantly. "I have to take you home, and I have to be downtown at eleven anyway. I feel fine, D.J."

Dani conceded, at least partly. "But you must promise that you'll let me know if you feel the least bit uncomfortable."

"It's a deal," Marcie said. "Now let's go or we'll get caught in traffic you won't believe."

Dani glanced at her watch when Marcie let her out of the car. She hurried along the sidewalk, fumbling for her apartment key. Marcie might make it to the office on time, but she was going to be late.

The kitten waited at her door, irate and persistent in his attempts to attract her attention.

"Oh, good grief," she said as he wrapped himself around first one ankle and then the other, and then she noticed that both his food dish and his water dish were empty.

"Come on," she said, opening the door and following him into the apartment. Stale, she thought when she closed the door, but the air in the apartment wasn't really stale. Shut up all weekend, the odors she noticed earlier had intensified. She wouldn't have been surprised had Nick walked around the corner from the bedroom, so poignant were the reminders of him surrounding her. She leaned weakly against the door.

"I am definitely going to have to air this place out," she said.

The kitten mewed his agreement from the breakfast bar but having done so renewed his complaints. She looked at him, sighed, and pushed herself away from the door. "All right."

She picked up the cat to put him outside and started to reach for the sack of cat food. "You're such a little fellow," she murmured, noticing how small he still was. She ruffled the fur under his chin and he purred appreciatively, settling himself in the crook of her arm. "Do you ever get lonely or afraid in that big world outside?" He licked at her arm, his tongue rough through the sleeve of her blouse.

"What am I doing talking to a cat?" She grabbed the sack of food and carried cat and food both to the front door. "I told you not to stick around here," she said. "I told you there wasn't anything here for you. Why didn't you listen to me?"

Marcie greeted her at the office with a thermal server of coffee and a handful of messages, most of them left over from Friday, but a few that had come in that morning. Dani carried them to her desk before she looked at them. Nothing important, she told herself, and then realized what she was looking for. Nothing from Nick. She hugged herself, grasping her upper arms, and rocked back in her chair. Hadn't she made it clear to him that she didn't want to hear from him? Abundantly, bitingly, cruelly clear? Then why was she sitting here mourning the fact that he believed her? *You're a fool, Dani Simms,* she told herself, *a fool for wanting what you're not meant to have.*

She pulled the telephone to her, sorted through the messages for the one she would answer first, and snatched up the receiver, but she hesitated a moment as, eyes closed, she held the receiver to her cheek. Then, with a determination she had to fight to maintain, she punched out the numbers for her first call. She had barely finished that conversation when Marcie entered with a stack of mail.

"It's Monday with a vengeance," Marcie said, grinning, handing her the mail and a sheaf of new telephone messages. "There's more mail, but I'm going to have to pull the files, and, if you don't mind, I'd rather do that after I get back from the doctor's office." She laughed. "The phone hasn't stopped ringing long enough for me to do it this morning."

"Did you call Chet and ask for someone to fill in for a while?" Dani asked.

"I tried, but no one answered his phone."

"That's strange." Dani pushed the mail to one side. "You hold down the fort while I see what I can find out."

Chet's outer office was empty. Although a large ring of keys rested on Robyn's desk, her typewriter was still covered, as was her calculator. Dani heard the soft murmur of voices through the slightly open door to the inner office. The door opened farther when Dani tapped on it.

Chet was seated at his desk, Robyn in the chair

across from him, crying quietly into a large white hand-kerchief. The young woman looked up, a silent "Oh!" forming on her lips, and Dani stepped back in embarrassment.

"I'm sorry, Chet. Marcie tried to call. Would you mind getting in touch with me in the next few minutes?"

"No, D.J. Wait a minute."

"Mr. Davis, please!" Robyn rose hastily from her chair.

"All right," Chet said wearily. "Why don't you go to the lounge for a few minutes. But don't leave. I want to talk with you again."

Robyn scooted from the room, leaving Dani standing awkwardly in the doorway waiting for Chet to speak.

Chet picked up the stub of his cigar from the ashtray, taking special care as he relighted it. "Come on in and close the door."

"No, really, Chet. All I needed was a temporary fill-in for Marcie's desk. I can tell this is a bad time. We'll get by without one."

"Please, D.J.," he said, sighing. "I think I need someone else's opinion. I'm having trouble being objective about this."

Dani glanced at the outer office as she closed the door. "It has to be something more serious than a fight with her boyfriend, then?"

"Yes."

She took the chair Robyn had just vacated.

"Robyn quit her job this morning."

Dani looked around his spotless office. "Why?" she asked. "She's been so good at it, and she seemed to enjoy it."

"The boyfriend," he said slowly, "the one I was afraid was going to marry her and carry her off?"

"Yes?"

"She said she found out this weekend that he was only using her to try to get information."

"Wonderful fellow," Dani said, feeling disgust tightening her stomach as she sank back into the chair. "Is she sure?"

"As sure as she can be. She said at first she thought he was only sharing her enthusiasm for her job, but that he had begun to ask some pointed questions, and finally he demanded that she go into a specific file."

"Did she?"

"No. And apparently they had quite an argument because she didn't."

Dani sighed and shook her head. "I can't imagine anyone using a woman like that. What could he have hoped to learn?"

"She wouldn't tell me."

"Are you trying to decide whether you should talk her out of quitting?"

"D.J., look around you. This is the first time this office has ever been organized. Things are finally where they're supposed to be. I can find them when I need them. And she's a delight to have around." He ground his cigar out in the ashtray. "Damn it, I don't want to let her go!"

Dani glanced toward the credenza in front of his window. One well-tended dracaena occupied the space formerly given to stacks of files.

"Was there a breach of any client's confidence?" she asked. "Or was the firm jeopardized in any way?"

"She says she doesn't think so. She believes that

whatever information she may have let slip, if any, was harmless."

"Is he going to be able to pressure her into doing what he wants at some later date?" Dani asked.

"No." Chet was emphatic. "She told me that she would never see him again, and I believe her."

"Then why are you having trouble deciding? She's going to punish herself for her error in judgment. You don't have to help her by accepting her resignation. As far as I can see, that's the only mistake she's made since she's been here, and she's not about to repeat it."

Chet nodded in agreement, and Dani realized he had only wanted his opinion reinforced. Well, why not? she wondered. No one but Robyn had been hurt.

"Now," Dani said, "about the reason I came down here."

"A temporary." Chet pulled a folder from his top drawer. "How long do you need her?"

"I'm not sure, but I hope for only a couple of hours."

It was long after lunch when Dani heard Marcie's voice in the hall and called her into her office.

"Well? What did the doctor say?"

Marcie grinned at her. "I'm fine, D.J., and the baby's fine. The reason it took so long is that he had to work me in. I told you there wasn't any reason to worry."

Dani hugged the woman. Maybe she hadn't meant to let herself care for her, but she did, and maybe she hadn't meant to let herself worry about anyone again, but she had. She pulled away.

"And is that all he said?" she asked sternly.

"No." Marcie laughed. "He did say I was going to have to find a better way to feed the dogs."

The time she had spent waiting for Marcie to return had dragged by, and now the afternoon seemed to go on interminably. The relief secretary had been assigned to her for the balance of the day, and Marcie took full advantage of the extra help to tackle the work that never seemed to be caught up. Dani knew that she should have been able to do the same.

And why couldn't she? It wasn't because of the dull headache throbbing in time with the clock, although she would have liked to blame it on that.

Admit it, Dani, she told herself in disgust. *Admit that you wish you hadn't told Marcie to return Nick's escrow file to Henry Slayton. Admit that you want to be the one to go with Nick tomorrow morning. Admit that you'd snatch at any excuse to see him one more time. Admit it and then forget it and get back to work.*

So she admitted it, hating herself for the weakness that made it true, but she couldn't forget it, and she couldn't get back to work.

Where was the excitement, the thrill of challenge that she used to feel? She looked around her at the neat stacks of work awaiting her. Today she couldn't see them as symbols of her growing professional reputation, or of her clients' confidence in her ability. Today they were just stacks of dry words and dusty pages stretching endlessly before her, filling her days, but not with joy, not with laughter.

She felt someone watching her, looked up from the contract that for at least half an hour she had been trying to read, and saw Frank Merriweather standing in her doorway. She blinked her surprise and rose hastily from the chair.

"Mr. Merriweather?" she stammered. "If I'd known you wanted to talk with me, I would have come to your office."

He closed the door and crossed the short distance to her desk. "Not if you'd known what I wanted to talk about," he said as he dropped a familiar, fat folder on the smooth surface in front of her.

She stared blindly at the folder, tracing one finger along the edge of the tab, as she felt her throat tightening. "This isn't necessary," she said slowly.

"It shouldn't be," Frank Merriweather insisted. "Nick isn't proud of what happened, but he would tell you about it if you'd give him an opening."

You want to know about Marilyn? Let me tell you about her. Dani covered her eyes with one hand. It was impossible. If she blocked out Merriweather's piercing gray gaze, she saw Nick's emotionless green one. "I know," she said.

"D.J.," the man's voice softened. "What are you afraid of? Nick is in love with you."

Because I loved you, Dani.

"No," she said solemnly, raising her head and looking directly into those gray eyes. "No, he isn't. He thought he was, but he didn't know me." Her voice failed her. "He can't love someone he doesn't know."

"And can you, D.J.?" Merriweather asked relentlessly.

"What?"

"Can you love someone you don't know?"

"That isn't fair," she whispered.

"Perhaps not," he said. "But perhaps nothing I've done in connection with you has been fair."

"You gave me back my life."

"Did I?" He shook his head. "I'm not sure now. When John Matthews called me about you, he was certain that time, and moving away from Oklahoma City and the memories it held for you, and starting over in a new, challenging job were all you needed to snap you back to your old self. I had placed so much emphasis on work in my life, it seemed reasonable to me. Besides, John swore you were the best intern his firm had ever had, your law school transcript was outstanding, and you'd done extremely well on the bar exam. I didn't see how anyone could be hurt by doing what John asked and giving you a job with this firm."

"If I've..." Dani heard only the resignation in his voice. She thought she had proved herself, but apparently she was wrong about that too. "If I've jeopardized the firm by my—involvement—with Nick, of course I'll leave."

"And go where?" he snapped. His voice softened. "One of these days, you're going to have to face whatever it is you're hiding from.

"No, I haven't been fair with you," he went on. "To have been fair would have been to deny you the chance to hide yourself in this job. To have been fair would have been to insist you continue with counseling sessions. To have been fair would have been to look behind that confident facade you've so carefully erected and see that you are still the same frightened, hurt little girl I first met five years ago."

"I'm not." Where was her voice? And what kept her behind this desk, unable to move, unable to fight his accusations, unable to do more than watch warily as this calm, understanding man quietly but uncharacteristically chiseled at the confidence she had worked so long to build?

"It's been five years. Five years, D.J.! Are you any closer to accepting your loss now than you were then?"

"I function," she said.

"Function?" He swore softly. "Computers function. I hope to God humans have more to look forward to than that."

"What do you want from me?"

"I want to see the person John Matthews assured me you were," he said steadily. "I want to see the woman who had enough enthusiasm and love to share with a husband and a child, a home, school, and a job. I want to see the woman who tackled life as if it were a game and found something to laugh about even when she didn't win."

It seemed so long ago. Had she ever really been that person? "Mr. Matthews couldn't have known that," she said.

"Couldn't he have? He knew that and more. You had a place with his firm if you could have brought yourself to stay in Oklahoma City. Instead," he said, sighing, "you came here, and I gained a competent automaton.

"I kept looking for the laughter. I kept thinking it was only a matter of time before I saw the woman John told me I was hiring. I had just about given up when I caught a glimpse of her, but now you're doing your damnedest to make sure no one ever sees her again. And I don't know why."

He sat in the chair across from her. She tried not to

look at him, this man who had been a friend when she needed one, who had never questioned her, who had given her a chance to reclaim herself.

"Mr. Merriweather," she said softly, "you did help me."

"Did I, D.J.? Or did I help you into a position to be hurt more?"

The folder sat squat and ominous between them. Once again she traced the outline of the tab.

"Nick has shown me what kind of person he is," she said. "I don't need to read Marilyn's bitter accusations. I've heard them from her. And if there ever was any truth in them, there isn't now."

She pushed the folder to one side. "Nick's past has nothing to do with what I am or who I am."

"And what about his future?"

She smiled a tight, painful little smile and said in a voice that sounded remarkably normal, "Nick's future doesn't include me."

"Even though you're in love with him?"

She stared at him silently. Could she ask him to leave? Could she tell the man who owned the desk behind which she sat, who owned the law books lining her walls, to leave? Could she walk out, knowing that if she did she walked out of more than an uncomfortable interview, she walked out on a man who had shown his trust in her, she walked out on her job, and maybe even her career? Now she knew why he had come to her office instead of asking her to his.

Merriweather rose agilely from the chair and paced to the window. "Nick's complete story isn't in that file. It ought to be, but he wouldn't let me use it."

"Please," she said. "Don't go on."

He studied her for a moment, shook his head, and continued. "When Nick first came to me wanting to divorce Marilyn, all he told me was to pay her whatever it took to get her out of his life, but he did warn me that the lawsuit could get messy. Nick has always had an explosive temper, and I wasn't surprised that she had finally provoked it. I was surprised when Marilyn countersued naming cruelty as her grounds, and Nick refused to give me any ammunition with which to fight her charges. At first he would say only that she was wise to be afraid of him, because if he was ever alone with her again, he might kill her."

Dani thrust her hand across her mouth to stifle a moan. Nick? Not the Nick she knew!

"He must have had a reason," she whispered.

"Yes, he did, and Marilyn knew he would never tell the court the real reason. She used that knowledge like a weapon. When he acceded to her first demand for a property settlement without a fight, she decided she wanted more. When he agreed to that, she wanted still more.

"Aren't you even going to ask me what the reason was, D.J.?"

Dani stared at him, unable to speak, unable to imagine anything horrible enough to have pushed Nick to that point.

Merriweather stood in front of her, both hands on her desk, leaning toward her. "Ask me, D.J. Not asking won't make it any less real. Not asking won't keep it from touching you. For God's sake, if you care about Nick, ask me."

And even as she was dragging her head to one side to deny she cared, her lips shaped the word, "What?"

He straightened and threw his head back, breathing deeply before he looked back at her and spoke softly. "Marilyn aborted Nick's child."

She was caught, suspended between breaths, between thoughts, between heartbeats until the softly spoken words exploded across her consciousness. "Oh, dear God," she moaned.

Nick's wife had done that? She saw Nick as he had helped her with Jennifer, as he had lovingly interacted with Timmie, and she thought of how much his family meant to him. How could he have borne it? *What did you do to your son?*

"Tim was at their house when Nick learned the truth," Merriweather continued quietly. "He heard them arguing and managed to get between them, managed to control Nick long enough for Marilyn to get out of the house. And Nick bought his divorce—not because of what he had done, but because of what he was afraid he would do."

He looked steadily at Dani. She pulled clenched hands from her lips and spread them on the polished surface of her desk, extending her fingers, watching but not seeing them.

"It wasn't easy for him to get through that time," he went on, "but Nick is a survivor. He didn't let the pain of his loss or the betrayal destroy him. And having suffered that kind of hell himself, do you really doubt that he would understand what you've been through?"

She couldn't answer him. *You'll tell me your horrible little secret and then I'll tell you mine.* She had said that, had said all of those things to hurt him, but, dear Lord, she had meant only to defend herself, not to wound him the way she must have.

"It's too late," she whispered.

"Only if you let it be. You didn't deserve what happened to you. You can't make it not have happened, but you can put it where it belongs. In the past. Those kinds of memories will always be a part of you, D.J., but they shouldn't control you. *Now* is for living.

"Why can't you let yourself love him, Dani?" She raised startled eyes when his voice softened perceptibly with her name. "Why can't you let him love you?"

Why couldn't she? She heard that question during the long drive home. She had been so certain he wouldn't love her, couldn't love her, that she set about to insure that he didn't. Well, he wouldn't, couldn't, didn't now, but having proved herself right brought no satisfaction. It brought instead a dull ache growing steadily within her.

She threw open the door to her apartment and let the kitten go in before her, strangely relieved to have even feline companionship when she entered. Nick's presence was indelibly stamped on the empty apartment. She stood quietly, head thrown back, absorbing it for long minutes, before she snapped herself into action. She went briskly through the apartment, opening drapes and windows and setting the thermostat control to blow fresh air through the rooms. She stripped the bed and covered it with clean sheets, not looking at the old ones as she stuffed them into the hamper, not letting her mind linger on the last time she had lain between them.

In the kitchen the kitten waited for the milk Nick would have given him. "Why not?" Dani said. She sighed, acknowledging that it would take more than airing the apartment to free herself from memories of

Nick, more than changing the sheets, more than telling herself it was over.

She made coffee and carried a mug of it into the living room. The kitten, replete after finishing his milk, crawled onto her lap as she curled into her corner of the couch. She lifted her hand to brush him away but let it drop carelessly to his back. He settled against her, his soft purring hypnotically comforting. Idly she ruffled the fur along his back. He was so small, so defenseless, and despite what she had said, so dependent on her.

She let her hand slide from him and in protest he stretched, placing his paws on her chest, claws extended, making soft kneading movements against her. She watched his paws, fascinated. His motions were so similar to her own. His little paws gripped and extended, gripped and extended as though to a metronome. She found herself duplicating the exercises with her free hand.

"Oh, kitten," she said, sighing, as she gathered him close and buried her face in his fur. "You've picked the wrong person. You need someone who can comfort you and play with you and love you. Just as I do," she whispered. "Just as I do."

Just as she had so briefly had, she admitted to herself. Suddenly Nick's presence was overpowering. She felt him beside her on the couch, the couch where they had first made love. She heard his laughter coming from the kitchen as he coaxed her to try his "cheap imitation" eggs Benedict. Not even the blue mug in her hand was free of memories. She saw him raising it to her lips as he held her, drowsy and satisfied.

"Damn!" she said. "I won't go through this. I won't!"

She scrambled from the couch, dumping the startled kitten to the cushions, and stormed into the kitchen. She tossed the contents of the cup into the sink and searched under the cabinet until she found a box of garbage bags. She shook out the black plastic bag. In went the blue cup. In went the second blue cup. She marched back into the living room, carrying the bag with her. In went the two homespun covered throw pillows. In went the alabaster ashtray. After a return trip to the kitchen, in went the two stemmed wineglasses, the bottle of Glen-whatsits, and the kitchen ashtray. She stalked into the bedroom. In went the ashtray from the bed table. In went the newspaper with the story of the Brady Center dedication. She glanced around the room, searching for anything else that had come into her house because of Nick. There was only—she jerked open the closet door. In went the low-heeled shoes, the jeans, and the blue gauze blouse.

She twisted the top of the bag, knotted it, and snatched up the bag to carry it to the trash. She got as far as the front door but could go no farther. "Not yet," she whispered. She leaned her head against the door. She would have to trash them. Otherwise, they would be just so much weight, dragging her down, tangible evidence of the brief time she had almost dared to dream. But did she have to do it now?

She put the bag in the back of her closet. The skirt of the russet silk hid it from sight. Hesitantly she smoothed the folds of the dress. It probably ought to go, too. But not now, she thought weakly. That was something she could decide—in a little while.

With night the air turned cool. Dani closed the windows and drapes and set the thermostat for heat, but she couldn't seem to drive out the chill. The telephone sat silently on her desk, but she found herself watching it as warily as she had when it terrorized her with its ringing. He won't call, she told herself, knowing there was no reason for him to call her. Now or ever, hadn't those been her words? But she lifted the receiver once, just to confirm by listening to the mocking dial tone that the telephone was working.

The kitten curled contentedly against her on the couch, his purring the only sound in the now dark room, and suddenly it wasn't enough. She had to hear another person's voice, had to talk to someone, or run screaming from the emptiness she had made for herself. But who? Nick! she cried to herself. But she couldn't call him. He would never again want to hear from her. There was nothing she could say that would erase what she had done. And she had no one else. No one—except—

She switched on a light and reached for the telephone. She hesitated for a moment and then punched out the numbers. She held her breath as the phone rang and rang and rang until a cheerful voice answered.

"Marcie?" Dani said quickly. "I—I wanted to be sure—I wanted to check to see if you're feeling all right."

Chapter Twelve

Dani dragged herself to work the next day, hollow-eyed and with a dull headache. As the sky had begun to lighten that morning, she had finally fallen into a fitful sleep, had slept through the ring of her alarm clock and had awakened with barely enough time to throw on clothes and makeup, pin her hair back, and fight traffic downtown. The day didn't promise to get any better either. The temperamental Oklahoma weather seemed to have tired of spring. Gray skies dripped a chill drizzle, not quite rain, but piercingly sharp when thrown by a gust of wind.

By the time she reached her office, she was damp and chilled and wishing that for once she had been able to roll over and stay in bed. Her first sight of Marcie chased that thought from her mind. The woman sat hunched over in her chair. One hand covered her eyes, and the other held her side, as her slender body shook.

"Marcie!" Dani hurried to her. The woman spun around in her chair and peered at Dani through the fingers of the hand that covered her face. Then Dani saw that it was laughter, not sobs, that racked her.

It sounded as though she said, "A cow chip, D.J.?"

before clasping both hands to her mouth to silence her laughter.

Dani tossed her purse on Marcie's desk and reached across her for the thermal server. Puzzled, but relieved that the woman was only enjoying a joke that, sooner or later, she would share, Dani poured a cup of coffee and waited for Marcie to bring herself under control. She sipped her coffee and studied Marcie while she waited. Had she heard correctly? Marcie had ways of finding out almost anything, but what could she have learned about that afternoon of idiocy?

Soon Marcie's shoulders stilled. She giggled one more time as she looked at Dani.

"All right," Dani said slowly, "are you going to let me in on what's so funny, or am I going to have to guess?"

"The oil page..." Marcie said, pointing to the newspaper on her desk and surrendering to another fit of giggles.

Dani picked up the newspaper. She drew in a quick breath and stared at the page as her heart pounded in tempo with her throbbing head. There, above the story that accompanied the county by county listing of wells staked and completed, the boldfaced headline taunted her. "Nick Sanders No. 1 Dani's Cow Chip Red Fork Producer."

Dani clutched the newspaper, rose to her feet, and walked silently into her office, closing the door behind her. Some time later she raised her head from her desk. There wouldn't be any picket fence and climbing roses now, but at least Nick had found his illusive Red Fork channel. At less than two thousand feet they had drilled into it, the article reported, and had stayed in it for an additional seventy-five feet. The well was flowing four hundred barrels of oil a day. It deserved headlines, even without the ridiculous name he had tagged onto it. Would the name haunt him, she wondered, the way it would haunt her?

But how appropriate, she thought, smoothing the newspaper. The same day he formally relinquished one dream seemed a fitting day to announce the achievement of another. It was a shame that neither Sam Wilson nor Marilyn would know that this well might not have been drilled if they hadn't attempted that shoddy trick with the Beckham County leases.

Beckham County leases! She had almost forgotten. She pushed up from her desk and ran across her office, calling out as she opened the door, ''Marcie, did you remember to tell Henry—''

Her words hung in midair as she grasped the door frame. Standing in the hall, wearing what he had once laughingly described as his ''banking uniform,'' a dark suit, conservative shirt and tie, but looking as though nothing could ever again make him laugh, stood the owner of Creek County's newest oil well.

His unruly hair looked as though he had been running his hands through it, and Dani fought down an insane urge to smooth his hair, to soothe the deep lines that creased his face making him look as weary and haggard as she felt.

She moistened her lips and swallowed, trying to ease the dryness in her throat. ''Hello, Nick.''

He stood watching her, without moving, without smiling, but his voice was soft when he spoke. ''Hello, Dani.''

She couldn't let go of the door facing, couldn't take a

step, either forward or back into the safety of her office. She could only look into somber green eyes that studied her unwaveringly.

"Congratulations on the Cow Chip," she managed to say.

"I had help."

She closed her eyes as memories of the afternoon they had staked the well overpowered her.

"Well," she said, remembering the only reason he could have for being here. "Henry Slayton is going with you for the escrow closing this morning."

"No, he isn't."

He wasn't making it easy for her. But then, she wondered, why should he? She clutched the door facing even more tightly. "Nick, you are his client. The only reason I became involved in this case is that he went on vacation. He should be with you today."

"No, he shouldn't."

She stared up at him helplessly, unable to voice any of the myriad thoughts spinning through her mind, begging to be spoken.

"You started this," he said distinctly. "You'll be there for the finish."

Before she could respond, he turned to Marcie. "Do you have the file?"

"Sure, Nick," she said, handing the folder to him.

Sure, Nick? Marcie, the soul of propriety when a client was anywhere in sight, had actually said, *"Sure, Nick?"* Dani's startled glance caught the bright smile Marcie flashed to Nick as she handed him Dani's purse, too. Traitor!

Nick thrust her purse at her and grasped her by the

elbow, leading her, stunned and unprotesting, down the hall.

"And after we finish this bit of unpleasant business," he told her in a voice pitched low so that no one else could overhear, "you and I are going to have a long talk."

And she knew what he wanted to talk about. But what could she say? *I'm sorry* seemed pitifully inadequate for the biting words she could never take back, and yet it was all she could say.

"About Friday," she began hesitantly.

"Later," he said tersely. "After we finish with Wilson."

The blue Mercedes, top securely in place, waited in the loading zone in front of the office building. Nick's fair-weather car had apparently seen its share of foul weather since Friday, Dani thought as she looked at the mingled red and gray mud covering the car. The only clean spots were on the windshield, where the wipers had kept the glass clear, and the cleanliness emphasized the pastel pink of the parking ticket stuck under the wiper.

Nick unlocked the passenger door, tossed a garish orange merchandise bag from the front seat to the back, and stepped aside to allow Dani to slide into the car. He handed her the folder, slammed her door, plucked the ticket off the windshield, and eased his length into the car without saying a word. He started the engine and shot out into traffic. The silence in the car was deafening. Almost as though he realized it, too, he turned on the radio, tuning in an easy listening station, but when the romantic strains of a familiar melody filled the car, he snapped off the radio, leaving only the rhythmic thumping of the windshield wipers to emphasize the silence.

The parking lot, shared by the bank and the adjacent shopping mall, crawled with cars even at this early hour. Nick finally found a parking space some distance from the entrance. Dani didn't wait for him to walk around to help her out. She met him at the front of the car. Once again he took her by the elbow and hurried her along.

Inside the bank he bypassed the long row of tellers' windows and went directly to the offices. He announced himself to the receptionist, who smiled apologetically.

"I'm sorry, but Mr. Wilson isn't here yet, and Mr. Tankersly, the trust officer, is still tied up in a meeting. He did say, though, that if you got here before he returned, to ask you to wait in his office." She showed them to the office. "I'm sure he won't be long, but would you care for coffee while you wait?"

"No. Thank you," Nick said, smiling politely, but he lapsed once again into stony silence when the woman left. He sank into a chair, obviously impatient and irritated by the delay and lost in thoughts far removed from this bank.

Dani watched him hesitantly for a moment and then sat in the chair next to his. The folder was a solid reminder of why they were together. Think business, she told herself, and when she did, she remembered Wilson's second underhanded sale of the leases.

"Nick?"

His head jerked up.

"Did you see Sunday's paper?"

He shook his head. "I haven't had time for a newspaper in days. Why?"

"Then you don't know about—"

Sam Wilson's laugh filled the room. He stood in the doorway, flirting outrageously with the blushing receptionist.

"Know about what?" Nick asked.

"Mid-South," Dani whispered, just as Wilson entered the room.

Dani felt a shiver of distaste run through her as Wilson nodded coolly to them and settled himself comfortably on the edge of the desk.

"It seems a shame to have to wait any length of time for what is little more than a formality," he said.

He was going to bluff his way through it, Dani thought, and Nick had no idea of what was going on.

"Does that mean you were unsuccessful in meeting our requirements?" she asked in a voice edged in ice.

"Unfortunately," Wilson said, smiling ruefully at her.

That poor excuse for a man ought to be put through at least a little discomfort, but without just blurting out what she knew, she had no way of letting Nick know what had happened. She played for time and a way to tell him. She gazed at Nick, praying he could read the silent plea for understanding in her eyes before she again spoke to Wilson.

"Perhaps we could all save some valuable time by rescheduling this appointment for a later date," she said.

She had Wilson's attention now, and Nick's.

"I believe my time for meeting your title requirements has expired," Wilson said tightly.

"Yes, it has," Dani told him, opening her folder. Marcie, ever efficient, had tucked a new legal pad and a pen inside the folder. Dani drew circles on the pad while she gathered her thoughts. "However, under the terms of the escrow contract, Mr. Sanders has an additional fifteen days to attempt to resolve those problems before relinquishing any claim to the leases."

Wilson's pale complexion grew even paler, and small beads of perspiration dotted his upper lip.

"What's your game, lady?" he asked tensely. "A month ago you told me this was an either-or situation. Either I came up with a farm-out agreement or you didn't take the deal. Why have you changed your mind now?"

Dani read the same question in Nick's eyes, but he said nothing. She played absently with the legal pad and as she did, she turned it over, exposing the top document in the file. She slanted the folder so that Wilson couldn't see the contents. Bless Marcie's organized, competent heart! Paper clipped to the escrow contract was the article from Sunday's paper, the incriminating paragraph circled in red ink.

"Your comment about 'welching' on a deal distressed Mr. Sanders greatly," she said sweetly, ripping the entire document from the file as she watched the vein in Nick's temple throb a warning.

"Perhaps you'd like to refresh your memory of the terms of the contract," she said to Nick as she handed him the papers, held so that Wilson saw only the backs of them.

"Perhaps I should," he said, his gaze probing hers before he glanced at the clipping. If possible, his already grim countenance hardened as he read the damning paragraph, but when he looked back at her, his eyes sparkled with understanding and appreciation.

Nick folded the contract in half and leaned back in his chair, facing Wilson. "I've had a little luck since the last time we met, and since you are indirectly responsible for that luck, I feel I owe you something."

Dani set her purse and file on the desk top and turned to watch Wilson's discomfort. She didn't know how far Nick would carry this line, but he was doing it beautifully.

"You don't owe me anything, Sanders," Wilson edged off the desk. "All I want to do is conclude our business and put this entire unpleasant experience behind us."

"But that wouldn't be fair to you, Sam," Nick said, smiling easily. "The leases have been tied up so long now that you won't have a chance of selling them to anyone else before they expire. Let me approach Mid-South. Maybe I can work something out with them. If not..." he hesitated and then smiled brilliantly. "If not, just to show my goodwill, I'll take a part of the acreage as a business risk."

"No," Wilson said. "No. You told me at our last meeting—"

"I said a lot of things at our last meeting," Nick said, looking at Dani while he spoke, "things said in anger that I've had time to reconsider." He drew his gaze from her and squared his shoulders as he faced Wilson. "In spite of what was said, this contract"—he tapped the document against his knee—"gives me the right to an additional fifteen days, and I intend to exercise that right."

Wilson's pale face was now tinged with green. Defi-

nitely green, Dani thought. She was so caught up in
appreciating his discomfort that she didn't anticipate
his move. Neither did Nick. Wilson's hand snaked out
and snatched the contract.

"Let me see that damn thing," he hissed, flipping
the pages open and stopping in frozen silence.

Wilson glared at her then, a look filled with such ma-
levolence that she involuntarily shrank back in her
chair, aware for the first time that this man could be a
dangerous enemy.

"You bitch," he spat at her. "You've done it to me
again."

Dani saw Nick's knuckles whiten as his hand clenched
into a fist. Quickly she placed her hand on his, urging
him by her light touch not to carry through with his intended action.

"I've merely done my job, Mr. Wilson," she said
carefully, feeling a little ashamed for taking credit for
what Marcie actually uncovered but knowing that now
was not the time to stop to give her credit. "Sometimes
it is necessary to pry behind the surface of something to
discover the truth."

"You will apologize to Miss Simms, Wilson." Nick's
voice cut across hers, deadly calm, but Dani was not
deceived. She felt his fist still clenched beneath her
hand.

Wilson visibly regained his composure. He looked at
her when he spoke, his eyes glittering brightly. "I think
not," he said concisely. "You aren't the only one who
can pry behind the surface."

Dani felt Nick's hand moving beneath hers, but she
was unable to look away from Wilson's mesmerizing
eyes.

"I think," Wilson continued, "that you will release this escrow contract today, and that you will keep your mouth shut about this entire transaction."

"Why would I do that?" Nick asked in a voice as cold as Wilson's.

Wilson smiled at her, a brittle, challenging smile. "Because your lovely lady has kept her secret so well, I don't think you would subject her to the embarrassment of having her clients discussing the months she spent in an expensive sanatorium with Frank Merriweather footing the bill. What was it, *Mrs.* Simms? Drugs? Alcohol?"

At first Dani couldn't comprehend what he was saying, and then her thoughts spun with the question of how he had found out, but even as she understood, as she silently formed Robyn's name, she heard a sound remarkably like a growl as Nick shook off her hand and sprang at Wilson.

She was paralyzed, unable to believe what she was witnessing, numb and senseless, until she realized that Nick's fist had connected with Wilson's jaw and that now he had him by the throat, his large hands choking the life from the man as he held him suspended against the wall.

"No! Nick, you can't!" she cried, running to his side, tugging desperately at his arm. She made no more impression on him than a fly would have. His eyes glazed with a fury she had never seen; he held Wilson, not hearing the man's attempts to call out, not hearing her words.

"He's not worth it!" she screamed at him, trying to pry his hands loose. And then, sensing nothing else could stop him, "It's true."

Somehow she had reached him. He released his grip on Wilson and let the man slide down the wall. He turned to her, his eyes still dazed but infinitely sad. She backed away from him, feeling the soft leather of her purse brush against her as she leaned on the desk.

"It's true," she whispered.

Nick called out to her, his voice hoarse with an emotion she couldn't stop to identify, but she was beyond hearing him, acting only on instinct. Her survival depended on her not hearing him. She snatched her purse from the desk, dodged his outstretched arm, and pushed through the throng of people trying to crowd into the small office. And if she couldn't listen to his voice, she refused to listen to the voice within her, the one that derided her as she fled from the bank, the one that called her a coward for fleeing, the one that called her worse for leaving Nick to face the questions that must follow.

She burst onto the crowded sidewalk with no plan of escape. When she saw the early morning shoppers, most of them with heads bowed against the light rain, she knew she needed no plan. She mingled with them, hurrying along, knowing that if necessary she could lose herself in any one of the shops. A taxi pulled up to the sidewalk ahead of her, letting out a passenger, and Dani ran to it. She had no desire to be alone in the crowd.

"Where to, lady?" the driver asked as she scurried into the back seat.

Where to? Where could she go? There wasn't any place she belonged.

"Where do you want to go?" the driver grumbled from the front seat.

It wasn't where she wanted to go. It was the only place she could go. She gave him the address of the apartment.

Tightly drawn draperies effectively blocked what little sunlight struggled through the dripping gray sky and refused to allow it to penetrate the gloom of the apartment. Dani, her shoes kicked off and her feet tucked under her, curled in her corner of the couch. The kitten, for once hesitant about approaching her, curled on the opposite cushion, watching her as she mentally surveyed the destruction of her life. And she was the one who had destroyed it. She couldn't escape that knowledge any longer.

Her career was ruined, or would be by the time Wilson finished with her. She might be able to make some sort of living handling divorces or bankruptcies from a neighborhood law office, but never again would Win-Tech or any of her other clients be able to read one of her decisively worded opinions without questioning her judgment.

And her job was gone. She couldn't subject Frank Merriweather to the embarrassment her presence in his firm would cause him once Wilson began spreading his tales.

It would make no difference now that Frank Merriweather had acted only from kindness, that she had been unable to care for herself and had no one to turn to. She remembered herself as she had been when he first approached her—the uniform the sanatorium had provided, starched faded jeans, and cotton shirts no more individual or appealing than the hospital gowns she had worn for so long, and she, sunk so deep in despair that she didn't care how she looked or what she did, responding only slightly when they forced her into physical therapy sessions, not at all in counseling, until he burst into her life, giving her a reason to care, tempting her with this job. With the help of Chet Davis he had found her individualizing clothes and later this apartment.

It would make no difference that he was the one who had voiced the anger she couldn't express when he learned of Mrs. Simms's parting words, "Don't turn to me for help, Danielle. The State raised you. It can take care of you now." No. It would make no difference that he had offered financial help only when her insurance was exhausted and that she had repaid every penny. Nor would it matter that she owed a debt to him that could never be repaid.

And Nick. Ah, that was the worst of it. She'd never had a chance to tell him she was sorry. Now she never would. If she didn't understand what had happened, how could he? How could she explain to him that she had used his strength, used the love he offered, hiding in it, being nourished by it, taking from him, always taking, not realizing until it was too late that she loved him, that she was capable of loving. And the horrible things she had said to him. If she hadn't been so defensive, hiding, always hiding, she would never have lashed out at him, cutting into wounds that were every bit as deep and as painful as her own.

She stretched her arm across the back of the sofa and leaned her head against it. And today? Because of her, she had seen Nick's awesome temper unleashed. Because of her, he had been beyond caring that he might kill a man.

"Oh, God, Nick," she moaned, "what have I done? What have I done?"

She felt a raspy tongue against her cheek and opened her eyes to see the kitten perched on the back of the sofa, his face next to hers. "It's all right," she said, ruffling his still damp fur. "I'm sturdy. I'll get through this."

She put the kitten back on the opposite cushion and watched his little paws kneading the upholstery. "I've started over before," she whispered. "I can do it again."

But could she? She felt her own hands kneading the air, clenching and extending in the familiar exercises, and concentrated on the blank wall across from her, trying to blank her mind. Could she survive this? Could she fight to rebuild her life knowing it would be as empty as the last five years had been, would be forever empty, forever without Nick?

She mustn't think about that now. Now she must concentrate on survival. Now she must push back any thoughts that threatened her survival. She could think about them later, when it was safe, when it wouldn't hurt so much.

What am I doing? Her life was in shambles, she had destroyed a man's love for her, she had hurt him needlessly and cruelly, and now she was busy tucking away her pain, anesthetizing herself so that she could function as though none of it had happened. *It ought to hurt!* What kind of person was she? A normal person would feel the hurt, would let herself feel the hurt. *Oh, God,* she screamed in silent prayer, *just once,* just once *let me feel something honestly! Just once let me know that I can feel it!*

She forced her hands to be still. She spread them on the cushion in front of her and stared at them. "Unless someone cares enough about you to look closely," Nick had told her, "the scars aren't noticeable. And once he cares that much, he ceases to see them." Oh, Nick, if only those were the only scars. Would you have ceased to see the others? And as that question whispered through her mind, she felt her breathing deepen, she felt the hollowness expanding behind her eyes. Her chest was full, too full for her ribs to contain the pounding pressure hammering to be released. A constriction somewhere above her heart began pushing its way upward.

It was too much! She couldn't take it now, not yet. Instinctively she started to push it away. *No!* If pain were the only thing she could feel, she would feel it. *She would live.*

She felt tears in her eyes then, tears she had thought never again to shed, brimming over, scalding her cheeks, as a broken sob tore its way from deep within her, followed by another, and another, until she collapsed against the cushion, her hands tight fists on each side of her head, giving way to the grief which racked her—grief for the life she would never share with Nick, grief for the pain she had caused him. And still the sobs came, and the tears, too long dammed, refused not to burn her eyes. Grieving for *now* was not enough. Too much waited its turn. Rob, laughing, gentle Rob, dying while he worked to make someone else happy. And Bobby, blue-eyed innocent Bobby, who never had a chance to dream. Dani moaned against the sofa cushion as all her ghosts demanded and had their moment. Only then did she cry for herself, for Dani, frightened

and alone, for Dani who through her thoughtlessness
and carelessness and selfishness had caused it all. She
cried until drained, her body shaking with sobs until it
had no more strength, and then she lay weak and defenseless against the damp sofa while the kitten mewed
anxiously and caressed her salty cheek with its tongue.

She found the strength to slide her arm around the
kitten's body and draw him close to her, his softness
a stark and needed contrast to the numbness, the
blessed, peaceful numbness now overtaking her.

The pounding on the door summoned her from that
numbness. She knew who it had to be and shrank
against the sofa even before she heard Nick call out.

"Dani? Dani, are you in there? Dani, if you're in
there, open the door!"

She heard the doorknob being tried and held her
breath, thankful for the solid wooden door and sturdy
deadbolt lock.

She was doing it again! Hiding. Always hiding. That
was Nick out there. The Nick she loved. Nick, who had
loved her. Nick, who after all she had put him through
deserved at least one final opportunity to confront her.

She struggled from the sofa and stumbled across the
room. She had trouble making her fingers manipulate
the lock, and she finally drew the door open to see him
striding away—not down the sidewalk toward the parking lot, but across the courtyard.

"Nick." Her voice was a hoarse croak, but he heard
her. He stopped, seemed to steel himself, and turned.
His eyes devoured her as he walked the short distance
to her door, but no more than hers devoured him.

He had discarded his jacket and his tie, and his collar.

was open. For some reason he carried that garish
orange merchandise bag she vaguely remembered seeing in his car. He looked awful—haunted and angry—
and for a moment she was frightened.

"I was going for the pass key," he said, then stood
silently watching, waiting.

"Are you all right?" They spoke simultaneously, but
neither answered the question.

And although Dani knew there was no way she could
undo what she had done, she had to speak. "I'm sorry.
So very sorry," she murmured, and then she was in his
arms, the package in his hand pressing against her
back, but it was all right, because he was holding her,
and she never wanted him to let her go.

He tilted her head and cupped her face with his hand,
tracing his thumb across the salty wetness of her cheek.

"You never cried," he said with a touch of wonder in
his voice. "They told me that never once the whole
time you were in that place did you cry."

"You knew?" And that was all right too. She wanted
him to know, wanted him to understand why she had
said what she said, why she had done what she had.

"Not until yesterday afternoon." He pushed gently
and moved with her into the apartment, pausing only
long enough to close the door before leading her to the
couch. His package landed with a resounding thump on
the coffee table as he gathered her against him, holding
her as if he, too, never wanted to let her go.

"Dani, why didn't you tell me?" he whispered
against her hair.

"I couldn't. I couldn't tell anyone."

"You lived with that horror locked within you for all
these years and never talked about it with anyone?"

She shook her head against his chest.

"Lord in heaven," he said, drawing her more tightly into the safety of his arms. "No wonder you fought like a wounded animal."

When he tried to pull away, she murmured a protest, clutching at his shirt.

"I want you to sit down," he said firmly, and when she did, he dropped down beside her on the couch and draped his arm over her shoulder, holding her to his side.

She felt him draw a deep breath and sensed his hesitation when he spoke. "I didn't know where to start, but I was finally able to contact the Fire Department inspector who investigated the—the fire. I talked to your neighbors. The man who heard the explosion and pulled you out of the house still lives next door. I found out about the weeks you spent in Mercy Hospital. But that was all. No one could tell us what happened to you after you were released from the hospital. No one—until we found Rob's mother."

Dani stiffened at the mention of the woman. Maybe it was only her reaction that made her hear the bitter twist to his words, because there was no bitterness when he continued, only a deep sadness.

"I finally saw the pictures I demanded from you," he told her. He took her hand in his, weaving his fingers through hers, looking all the while into her eyes and compelling her to look into his. "Hundreds of pictures, but not one of you."

"There wouldn't have been," Dani whispered, able now to let the hurt show. "She never thought I belonged."

"Dani—" He seemed unsure of himself, debating

whether or not to do something. He was still hesitant when he reached across her and picked up the orange bag. He handed her the package almost apologetically.

"It didn't seem fair for her to have all that she had and for you to have nothing."

With trembling fingers, Dani reached into the sack and pulled out a slim white leather photograph album. Her hands were shaking so she could hardly open the cover. Snapshots. At least a hundred of them. Of Bobby as a baby, his wispy hair so pale it barely showed in the picture. Of Rob, beaming at his new son. Of Bobby, learning to crawl, learning to walk, learning to explore. And of Rob, there with him, teaching him, playing with him, laughing with him. The pain of her loss twisted through her as she turned the pages, until she turned the last one and closed the book, holding it firmly to her lap with both hands.

She hadn't quite shed the last tear. She felt them welling up again, felt her breath catching in her throat. She moaned once and then she was sobbing uncontrollably against Nick's chest, soaking his shirt, while he held her, while he rocked her and comforted her, until once again she was spent.

She drew a long, quavering breath but didn't raise her head from his solid support. "I loved them."

Nick smoothed stray tendrils of hair away from her face and lightly caressed her cheek. "I know."

She sniffed and burrowed her head closer to him.

"No one ever loved me before Rob," she said, at last able to talk. "He and Bobby were my life. I had everything I had ever wanted—love and a family and a home—and in the space of an afternoon it was all taken away. I couldn't understand why I was still alive. And I was so alone."

Nick tangled his fingers in her hair and pressed her head against him. She heard his words and felt them vibrate through his chest. "Rob may have been the first to love you, but, Dani, he wasn't the last. I can only imagine how alone you must have been—it's inconceivable that that woman could have abandoned you when you so desperately needed help—but that's over now. You'd be surprised how many people love you, and how many more would if you'd let them."

He spoke soothingly, as though to a child. "Marcie didn't hesitate a second when I called her Saturday morning. All she asked was how she could help."

"You called her?" Dani sniffed again and moved against him, at last understanding. "I wondered why she suddenly needed my help."

"I couldn't leave you by yourself, Dani." He tightened his arms around her. "And I was only hurting you by staying. I had to leave to find out what was tearing you apart."

She pulled away from him. "I didn't mean what I said to you."

"I know. Can you ever forgive me for pushing you to that point?"

Forgive him? Nick was asking her to forgive him?

"I know now what you must have been thinking," she said. "Mr. Merriweather told me...about Marilyn."

Nick sighed. "He shouldn't have. I should have been the one to tell you. But I suppose it was inevitable that he would. We called him yesterday afternoon from the sanatorium. Without his cooperation they would never have talked to us.''

Dani shifted against him, and the album slipped in her lap. She lifted it as though seeing it for the first time. ''Rob's mother would never have given me this,'' she said reluctantly.

''No. She wouldn't,'' he admitted.

''Then how—''

''The brothers Sanders can be formidable,'' he said, and it was obvious he meant to say no more, but Dani had no intention of pressing that question. She was too stunned by what he had said. ''We,'' he had been saying. ''Us.''

''Tim?'' she asked suddenly. ''Tim went with you? Tim knows?''

''Knows what, Dani?'' Nick questioned her sharply. ''He knows that you suffered a tragic loss. He knows that for a while the pain of that loss was more than you could bear. Why shouldn't he know that?''

He held her away from him, looking into her eyes. ''There's more, isn't there?'' he asked.

She shook her head, afraid to speak. ''I—'' She could remember so well now, all the things Rob's mother had said. ''She told me—'' She caught her hand to her mouth and rocked herself back and forth, hearing the words, letting herself hear the words that had clawed so long at her memory. ''God, how she must have hated me,'' Dani moaned. ''And I believed her. I didn't want to believe her, but I did. All these years.''

Nick stilled her rocking, his hands firm on her shoulders. ''What did she tell you, Dani? What else did that woman do to you?''

She stared at him, at the steel edge of anger reflected

in his eyes, and knew, intuitively, that it was not directed at her. Why had she never challenged those words before? Why had she been so afraid of letting them surface? She felt her own anger welling within her, clamoring to be let out.

"Damn her!" she cried. "It was *not* my fault!"

She felt Nick's hands clench on her shoulders. "She told you *that*?"

Dani nodded, remembering ... remembering. "Time after time. She was there every time I woke up—"

Nick spoke gently, interrupting her stammered words. "She poisoned you with her bitterness when you were too vulnerable to recognize what she was doing. Dani, it was an accident. No one is to blame for what happened."

"I know," she said. And she did. She knew it, and she *felt* it. "I know," she cried. "I know it now, Nick!"

She felt suddenly light and young and free. She threw her arms around Nick and hugged him close. "Thank you," she said fiercely. "Oh, thank you."

He circled her with his arms. "Why are you thanking me, Dani? You're the one who did all the work."

She hid her face against his neck and didn't answer. Now was not the time to tell him she wouldn't have gone through this if she hadn't thought she'd lost him.

He pushed her gently away. "Go wash your face," he said softly. "We're getting out of here."

She sat up with an embarrassed laugh and brushed at her cheeks. "I must look awful."

"No," he said, smiling at her. "But with my reputation, I don't want to run the risk of someone thinking I've been beating you."

"Oh." She clasped a hand to her mouth.

"Dani, I'm teasing."

"I know you are," she said. "But I just remembered Sam Wilson. Are you in a lot of trouble?"

"No," he said. "Wilson and I reached a compromise. One I can live with, and one he'd damned well better." He traced tentative fingers across her cheek. "And you're not in any trouble either. I know how much your career means to you. He won't do anything to jeopardize that."

She turned her face into his hand in a moment of silent gratitude, then she smiled hesitantly at him, not wanting to drop the subject but knowing that now was not the time for this discussion either.

He stood up and held his hand out to her. She clasped it and let him help her to her feet, wanting to walk into his arms but going instead toward the bedroom.

Her suit was crumpled beyond belief. She'd have to change. And why not change into clothes he preferred? She knelt by the garbage bag in the back of the closet, struggling with the knot until she freed it. She took out the jeans and gauze blouse and then shook her head. She had stuffed them into the bag with no thought of ever wearing them again, and now they were as impossibly wrinkled as the suit she wore. She folded them and placed them on the floor beside the bag. There would be another time for them.

She took slacks and a blouse from the rack and walked into the bathroom. The image that greeted her from the mirror did look awful, ravaged by tears, with red, swollen eyes. She turned on the cold water, splashing it against her face to try to take away some of the swelling. She thought she heard noises from the bedroom, but when she turned off the water, she heard nothing. Quickly she changed clothes and reached for her makeup. Makeup wouldn't help, she realized. But time would. Just as time would help the headache and the crushing weariness that had settled over her. Just as time would help heal the wounds between her and Nick. He cared for her. No one could have done what he did for her without caring. And if he cared for her there was hope—that he still loved her, or that he could love her again, and this time he would never doubt that she returned his love.

She noticed a subtle difference in the bedroom and in the closet, but she didn't stop to identify the difference. She remembered that her shoes were in the living room, beside the couch. Her stockinged feet made no noise as she entered the room, and she stood quietly, smiling, as she watched Nick playing with the kitten. A month before she had told the cat there was nothing here for him, or for her. How wrong she had been. As Nick bent to let the cat drop down to the coffee table, her gaze followed him and she saw her suitcase sitting beside the table.

"Where are we going, Nick?" she asked, praying for one answer.

He spun around to face her, a hesitant smile tugging at his lips. "You don't belong here anymore, Dani. I'm taking you home."

Home. Home with Nick. The closest thing to heaven she would know in this life. The answer she had prayed for. But now Nick, always so confident, seemed apprehensive. "If you want to go," he said softly.

"Oh, yes," she said, gliding to him as she had wanted to earlier, feeling his arms wrapping around her. "Oh, yes."

"Dani..." Still, he hesitated. "When you live with an alcoholic, as Tim and I did, growing up, you tend to color other persons' actions with your own memories. I didn't believe what I said to you, about drinking, any more than I believed what I said to Tim, but I was caught in my past. It was as though I had to draw those comparisons, even knowing they were wrong." He sighed deeply. "Tim and I had a lot of time to talk together this weekend. I finally convinced him to let someone else handle his case load so that he can have his vacation. That's really all he needs." His eyes pleaded with her for understanding. "My family is still at the house. If you think—if you'd rather not be with them now, I can take you somewhere else, anywhere else you'd rather go."

What was he really saying? Was he afraid she was not ready for his family, or was he afraid his family was not ready for her? She looked at him questioningly.

"They want you to be a part of us." His arms tightened around her. "I want you to be a part of me. But I know you still have things to sort out. Don't let what I want rush you into a decision you'll regret."

She put her fingers to his lips to silence him. Joy flooded through her with a sweetness she had never imagined. He did love her, and now, *now* was the time to tell him.

"I want to be with you," she said, "wherever you are... I love you, Nick."

She felt him release pent-up breath. "I know," he told her.

"You know?"

"I've known for weeks, but I was afraid you'd never realize it."

He bent to her then, and she went on tiptoe, wrapping her arms around his neck and arching into the curve of his body. She felt his hands in her hair, scattering pins as he loosened its waves to fall over her shoulders. He lifted her from the floor as their mouths met in a kiss so achingly full of promise she moaned and struggled closer to him. He turned with her, and she felt something solid beneath her feet. The coffee table. She thought fleetingly that they must forever make a place for that coffee table, and then she thought no more, because Nick was molding her to him, his hands as hungry for the feel of her as hers were for him, his mouth as hungry for the taste of her as hers was for him.

"God, Dani," he whispered against her throat, "I thought I'd lost you."

"Never, Nick," she promised. "Never, I—ouch!"

Nick pulled away from her, his glance following hers as she bent to her leg. The cat that was not her cat, too long ignored, was busy climbing the leg of her linen slacks. She lifted him up, disengaging his sharp little claws, and then brought him up to rest on her arm. He was still small, still defenseless, and still, she now accepted, dependent upon her.

She glanced a question at Nick. He laughed, gathering her and the kitten to him. "Yes, D.C., you can go too."

"D.C.?" Dani asked.

"Short for Dani's cat," he said. "You're going to have to call him something."

He lifted her from the coffee table, letting her slide down the length of him until her feet rested on the floor. She leaned against him, feeling the energy flowing between them, bonding them. His love was more than she had dared to dream for, but never again would she doubt it. She looked up at him, letting him read in her eyes the love she felt for him.

His smile was the sunshine that had been missing from this gray day. "Let's go home," he said.

Yours FREE, with a home subscription to
HARLEQUIN SUPERROMANCE ™

Complete and mail the coupon below today!

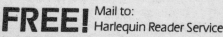

- -

FREE!
Mail to:
Harlequin Reader Service

In the U.S.
2504 West Southern Avenue
Tempe, AZ 85282

In Canada
P.O. Box 2800, Postal Station "A"
5170 Yonge St., Willowdale, Ont. M2N 5T5

YES, please send me FREE and without any obligation my **HARLEQUIN SUPERROMANCE** novel, LOVE BEYOND DESIRE. If you do not hear from me after I have examined my FREE book, please send me the 4 new **HARLEQUIN SUPERROMANCE** books every month as soon as they come off the press. I understand that I will be billed only $2.50 for each book (total $10.00). There are no shipping and handling or any other hidden charges. There is no minimum number of books that I have to purchase. In fact, I may cancel this arrangement at any time. LOVE BEYOND DESIRE is mine to keep as a FREE gift, even if I do not buy any additional books.

NAME _____ (Please Print)

ADDRESS _____ APT. NO.

CITY _____

STATE/PROV. _____ ZIP/POSTAL CODE

SIGNATURE (If under 18, parent or guardian must sign.)

134-BPA-KARV
SUP-SUB-11

This offer is limited to one order per household and not valid to present subscribers. Prices subject to change without notice.   Offer expires January 31, 1985

Get this book FREE!

Mail to:

Harlequin Reader Service

In the U.S.
2504 West Southern Ave.
Tempe, AZ 85282

In Canada
P.O. Box 2800, Postal Station A
5170 Yonge St., Willowdale, Ont. M2N 5T5

YES! I want to be one of the first to discover **Harlequin American Romance.** Send me FREE and without obligation *Twice in a Lifetime.* If you do not hear from me after I have examined my FREE book, please send me the 4 new, **Harlequin American Romances** each month as soon as they come off the presses. I understand that I will be billed only $2.25 for each book (total $9.00). There are no shipping or handling charges. There is no minimum number of books that I have to purchase. In fact, I may cancel this arrangement at any time. *Twice in a Lifetime* is mine to keep as a FREE gift, even if I do not buy any additional books.

154-BPA-NAXE